PAINFULLY
attractive
LOVE AND CARE

SILVIA VIOLET

Painfully Attractive by Silvia Violet

1

WREN

The doorbell rang, and Avery stood to answer it. I huddled further under the blanket he'd given me. Why had I been so stupid? Why had I told a man on a fucking app that I wanted to try pain play, then agreed to meet him at a sketchy-as-hell bar? Not at a place I knew. Not for coffee before trying a scene. I'd been so determined to overcome my fear and find someone who would give me what I wanted that I'd ignored everything I knew about safety.

The man had turned out to be an abusive asshole who didn't want to negotiate or even hear my hard limits. I'd had to fight my way out of the back room he'd lured me to. Thankfully, some of the bar's customers helped me, and once the asshole had been kicked out, I'd called Avery, my dad's boyfriend, and he'd come to pick me up. He'd even been nice enough not to berate me for being an idiot, and now he'd called my dad's best friend, Leo, to come talk to me. Apparently, Leo owned a kink club, and he also counseled people who'd had a bad experience with BDSM.

Avery was sure Leo could help me figure out how to get what I want without putting myself at risk.

I'd agreed to talk to Leo as long as Avery didn't tell him who I was. I doubted Leo would recognize me, since my dad and I hadn't been speaking during most of the time they'd known each other. It was only recently Dad and I had become close again, so if Leo had seen any pictures of me, they were probably from when I was a little kid. But my name was unique enough that if Leo had seen me before, it might jar his memory.

When Avery opened the door and I got a good look at Leo, my mouth dropped open. I'd seen pictures of him with my father, so I knew he was hot, but I wasn't prepared for my intense reaction to him. I let my gaze roam over his close-cut dark hair, his scruffy beard, his broad shoulders and thick, muscular body. But as gorgeous as he was, it was his presence that really drew me in. I'd never met anyone who screamed Dom quite so loudly. I wanted to beg him to hold me, because I knew he'd keep me safe.

I sat up straighter on the couch, realizing I'd stopped shivering for the first time since I'd fought off the asshole who wouldn't take no for an answer. Leo's presence calmed me before he'd even spoken, like my body knew him even if I didn't.

Avery followed Leo into the living room and gestured toward a chair. "Have a seat. This is——"

"Will. That's my name. Will." Wow, I sounded like an idiot who wasn't even sure of his own name. I prayed Leo would just think I was awkward or so shaken up I was failing at basic conversation. I'd been so worried Avery would forget and call me Wren that I'd jumped in with the first thing that came to mind.

Luckily, Leo didn't seem fazed by my awkwardness. He reached out his hand for me to shake. His grip was firm, but he made no attempt to assert his dominance, not that he needed to. His fingers grazed my palm when I let his hand go, and a jolt of electricity sizzled up my arm, making me jump.

"I'm here to help you any way I can," Leo said.

I'd been so consumed by the tingle he'd sent through me that I startled when he spoke.

"I'm sorry. Do you need some more time before we talk?"

"Oh, no. I… I was just lost in thought. It's okay."

Leo nodded. "If you want to press charges against your assailant, I can help you. If you want to talk about what happened, I'll listen. And if you just want to have someone stay with you, I'll be here. We can set up another time to talk later too, if that's better."

"Thank you… that's… I just appreciate you coming."

"You're welcome, and once you feel ready, I'll help you find a healthy way to explore what you're interested in."

"Yes, I'd like that… your help… finding… being able to…"

He smiled. "It's okay if it's not easy to find words right now."

I wasn't sure I'd have been able to talk properly around him under the best of circumstances, but even though he made me tongue-tied, I did want to talk to him. I knew instinctively that he would listen and not judge. Avery would too, but he was my dad's boyfriend, and I really didn't want to think about how he knew what he did about the BDSM scene.

I swallowed and tried to make my brain work. "I would like to talk about what happened and what I wanted to have happen and why I was so stupid. All that."

Leo nodded. "I'm here to listen, but you weren't stupid. You were taken advantage of. Yes, you should use caution, but that does not make what happened your fault."

Avery had said the same thing. I hoped eventually I'd be able to believe them. "Thank you."

"I'll go in my bedroom and leave you two alone," Avery said. I'd been so focused on Leo, I'd almost forgotten he was there.

Avery stood, and I looked up at him. "Thank you. For coming after me, for calling Leo, and for letting me take over your apartment."

"You're welcome. Take as long as you need. You can stay here tonight, or Leo or I will drive you home."

He left then, and I started talking, letting the words simply spill out. It was easier than I'd thought it would be, because Leo never seemed to be judging me or feeling sorry for me. He just listened and occasionally commented, seeming to know exactly the right thing to say at the right time.

My face burned with embarrassment as I stumbled through my confession that I was looking for a Dom who would help me experiment with pain play, but Leo gave me a reassuring smile.

"There is absolutely nothing wrong with you or with your desires. You just need a safe place to explore them. Avery was right to call me, because I can find that for you."

I couldn't remember a time I'd felt more comfortable with anyone I'd gone out with, male or female. I knew right then that I was in big trouble, because I didn't want Leo to find someone to help me. I wanted him to help me himself. I'd finally found the person who could give me what I needed, but he was my father's best friend, and I'd just lied to him about who I was.

2

LEO

I handed Will one of the cans of Coke I'd grabbed from the bar, then shut the door to my office. This was the third time we'd met, and I still hadn't shaken the sense that I knew him from somewhere. But that couldn't be. I would never forget meeting a man who pushed so many of my buttons with his curly, dark hair, soft brown eyes, and submissive desires. Maybe I'd just caught a glimpse of him here at my club.

I pushed away those thoughts. He was here because he'd been scared by someone who tried to take advantage of him. I needed to act like a compassionate professional, not a horny asshole. I didn't usually have trouble talking objectively about kink without becoming aroused, but today my cock hadn't gotten the message that this was an information session, not a scene.

"Are you comfortable here?" This was the first time we'd met at Thrust. He'd told me he'd come here a few times, but he'd been too nervous to approach anyone.

"Yeah… sure." He glanced around the room as he took a sip of his soda.

"You don't have to say yes. If you'd rather talk somewhere else, we can leave. I only suggested meeting at the club because as we talk about what you want to explore, I can show you some of the toys and implements we have here." Unfortunately, just mentioning toys had me imagining how he'd react to them. Maybe I needed to suggest he talk to someone else.

"It's fine, really. I trust you."

"Because Avery trusts me?"

He nodded.

"It's always good to ask around about anyone you're going to play with. The community here is small enough that if one person doesn't know the play partner in question, they probably know someone who does. It's never wrong to question."

"Yeah, I wish I'd done that. I wish I'd done a lot of things differently. I just… I don't know. I want to try pain play, but actually getting up the nerve to talk to somebody about it was harder than I thought it would be. So I decided it would be easier to just set up a scene through an app."

"I know talking about what you want can be intimidating, but it's still best to talk in person before agreeing to a scene, even if it's someone you initially met online."

He looked down, and I hated seeing such sadness in his expression.

"Do you want a candy bar?" I opened my desk drawer where I kept a stash of chocolate, my favorite thing to give a shaky sub after a scene.

He tapped the side of his soda can and studied me. "Are you trying to give me a sugar rush?"

I smiled. "No, I just want you to be comfortable."

"Thank you." He rose to peer into my drawer. "What have you got in there?"

"Milk chocolate and dark chocolate squares, Reese's cups—"

"Yes, one of those."

I smiled as I handed him one. "They're my favorite too."

"I don't guess you'd add whatever is in the flask I saw to my drink?"

"It's bourbon, and no. If you want to go out for drinks another time, we can, but we should stay sober for this talk." Then a disturbing thought hit me. Will had to be close to twenty years younger than me, but how young was he? "You are old enough to drink, right?"

He scowled at me. "Yes. I'm twenty-two."

I held up my hands. "Sorry. I just had to ask."

"I'm not a baby. I graduated from UNC-Asheville in the spring, and I've been doing a design internship for the summer. I've even been accepted to a graduate program at UNC-Charlotte, but I haven't decided if I'm going to go or not. Apparently, I need as much advice about my career as I need about"—he waved his hand around—"all this."

I grabbed a Reese's cup for myself as I answered. "It's okay to be unsure about what you want to do with your life and about what you want sexually. There's nothing wrong with exploration; not everyone knows immediately what they like in any aspect of their life."

He huffed. "Tell that to my dad." As soon as he said the words, he got an odd, almost scared look on his face. I wasn't sure how to read that.

"Is he pushing you to make a decision?"

"Yes, and I get it. Classes start in just a few weeks. He's even willing to pay for the program, but I'm just not sure."

Hmm. He didn't seem to have a bad relationship with his dad; maybe I was overanalyzing. "I own another club in Charlotte. It's a good place to live, and I love how downtown has developed in the last few years, but I can see why Asheville might be more attractive."

"So have you moved here, or do you still live in Charlotte?"

"I've been spending a lot of time here since I bought Thrust, but I live in Charlotte. I'll be there a lot more next month."

"Oh. So if I wanted you to teach me about pain play, you wouldn't be here to do it?"

I coughed, trying to cover up my surprise. Had I said something to make him think that I…

But you do want to teach him, don't you? Damn that seductive voice in my head. I couldn't stop myself from imagining all the things I wanted to do to Will. How would he react to a flogger? A crop? My favorite nipple clamps? Edgier things? I could see him stretched out for me, bound, begging for more. But no, I wasn't what he needed, no matter what my cock thought.

"Once we talk more specifically about what you're looking for, I'll help you figure out the best way for you to explore your desires safely, but that doesn't mean you'll be exploring with me. I don't really work with new subs anymore."

"Why not?"

That wasn't the question I expected, and I had no idea what to say. I couldn't tell him the raw truth, that the play I used to love had lost most of its excitement for me. How would it sound for a man who ran two kink clubs to say he wasn't sure he even liked kink anymore? But when I imagined being Will's Dom, I felt the same excitement I used to. Maybe I'd gotten into a rut, and what I needed was something new, someone different from the subs I usually took on. I needed someone I felt a real connection with. Someone like Will.

No. I was too old for him, too set in my ways, and too interested in more serious pain.

"I'm busy now, running two clubs. I don't really have time for training. I do demos and classes occasionally but nothing more long term."

"Do you have a partner?" He bit his lip as soon as the question was out. "I'm sorry. That was probably inappropriate."

"It wouldn't be if I was considering this arrangement." Was I considering it? "If I had a partner who would make demands on my time or who might be jealous, you'd need to know. But no, I don't."

He frowned. "That's hard to believe."

I was shocked when heat rushed to my face. When was the last time a man had made me blush? "Thank you, but trust me, just because you own a couple of clubs doesn't mean it's any easier to find a partner."

He sighed. "Then how am I ever supposed to do it?"

"First of all, you need to figure out what you like by playing with a few Doms. Then, hopefully, you'll meet someone compatible. I'm grouchy and overly picky. You may have a much easier time finding what you're looking for."

"You don't seem grouchy to me. You seem really kind. You dropped whatever you were doing and came to talk to me because I was scared."

Oh fuck. Hearing him sound so in awe had me really considering what he'd proposed. "Making sure people feel safe exploring their kinks is very important to me. So yes, I was willing to come right away when you needed me."

He gave a soft smile that threatened to melt my resistance. "Thank you."

"You're welcome. Now, let's talk about what you're looking for."

"You mean like what I want to do?" His teeth sank into his lip again. God, had I ever been that young and innocent? He was all fresh and new to this, and I wanted to initiate him. I wanted to see the mark of my hand on his ass. I wanted to make him cry out, to see his face when he orgasmed after I'd hurt him just as much as he wanted me to. But that wasn't a good idea. The things I enjoyed weren't for novices.

"Yes, that's what I mean, but you don't have to be too specific yet. First of all, do you want this to be a sexual relationship or only a D/s one?"

"I totally want my Dom to fuck me."

Oh my God. I might not survive this. "You know some people keep sex out of their scenes, and that's okay."

"I've read about that on BDSM sites, but I can't imagine it. Just thinking about being spanked or flogged or being forced to wear nipple clamps makes me hard."

Hearing him mention it made me hard as well, and that made me even more reluctant to turn him over to another Dom.

I took a deep breath. Was I really considering playing with him? Maaaaybe.

If we put a time limit on it, if I agreed to a specific number of sessions, then I'd know when the end was coming. It wouldn't come as a surprise like it had with the last boy I'd taken on. I'd thought things were going well. I'd thought he had deeper feelings for me. I'd been very wrong.

But if I wasn't wondering if things would continue like I had other times, I wouldn't be questioning if there could be more between Will and me.

Aren't you already questioning that? I really, really hated that voice.

"Before we discuss that further, I'm going to pull up a

list of activities you and your Dom could try. Some of these might be things you never want to do."

"Hard limits."

"That's right. Others you might not be sure about, and some you'll definitely want to try. Remember that trying something doesn't mean you have to like it. A good Dom will stop the moment you use your safeword. When you're done going through the list, we'll compare our interests."

He studied me for a moment. "So you are considering taking me on?"

Damn him. His coy tone went right to my dick. How the hell could someone so young and innocent be seducing me? Wasn't I too jaded for that?

If he could affect me this easily, he'd have far too much power over me if he actually offered me his submission. My traitorous mind created a picture of him on his knees, looking up at me with those dark eyes, trusting, patient, ready to take whatever I gave him. It was the most intoxicating thing I'd fantasized about in months. What was it about this man? Was this how Graham felt when he'd met Avery? He'd told me that a few minutes with Avery was all he needed to know that Avery was his.

No, that was not what was happening here. Graham and Avery had some kind of magic; what had happened to them was a one-in-a-million thing.

"Did I ask the wrong thing?" Will looked so nervous. Damn, he was still waiting on my answer.

"Sorry. I got lost in my thoughts. I was… just ignore me. I suppose I'm considering it, but I'm not sure it's a good idea."

"I know I'm pushing. Anyone who knows me will tell you how stubborn I am."

"Are you saying you're going to be a challenge to your Dom?"

He shrugged. "I'm not deliberately trying to be a bratty sub or anything, but wouldn't some level of challenge be fun?"

Yes. Yes, it would. Fuck. I should run as fast as I could. The sensible part of me was screaming that Will was trouble, but I wasn't listening. Instead of answering, I pulled up the list and handed Will my iPad.

"So what happens if our lists are compatible?" he asked, after glancing at the document in front of him.

Heaven help me. "Fill it out, and we'll see."

3

WREN

I was buzzing all over as I read through the list Leo had given me, and try as I might, I couldn't keep my reactions off my face. Some of the things on the list were downright scary. I couldn't believe people seriously wanted to do some of this stuff. But other things I read had me so hard I could barely think; at least, until I came to another hard no.

And every time I checked something or passed it by, I wondered how my answers would line up with Leo's. I really hoped we had similar interests, because I'd never wanted anyone like I wanted him.

You should tell him who you really are.

I should, but if he knew, he would never agree to play with me. I finally had a chance to explore all the things I'd fantasized about for years with a man I could trust. I didn't want to give that up, even if it meant keeping my secret. I glanced up and caught him staring at me. When I smiled, he looked down at the paperwork in front of him. I loved that he seemed affected too. He was so fucking hot, and I wanted his hands on me.

A few moments later, I came to the end of the survey. "I'm done."

Leo looked up. "Already? That's faster than I expected."

"I did skip a few things, because I wasn't sure what they were, even though I've done a lot of research."

"It's rare for anyone to know all the things on the list, no matter how experienced they are. I should have mentioned that."

"Oh, that makes me feel better."

"Good, but I don't want you to feel like you had to rush. Are you sure you don't need more time?"

"I'm sure. I have a few questions, but I can ask them as we see what we both like."

Leo narrowed his eyes. "You know we don't have to like exactly the same things to be compatible, right? We can just go through in order."

"But you said—"

"Are you sure you're not a bratty sub?"

I was really pushing, but I just wanted him so much. "I don't mean to be, but I guess I've always been trouble."

He frowned. "What kind of trouble?"

"I don't know. I'm the one who always makes a mess of things."

"Will, I don't think you're going to make a mess of this."

He sounded so certain, it made my chest warm and tight. "Really?"

He nodded as he held out his hand for the iPad. I gave it to him and tried not to squirm as he read through my answers. I was so nervous. I wanted him to agree to take me on. The longer I was with him, the more I was sure he was the right Dom for me.

Finally he looked up. "Your instincts were right. Our interests are very compatible."

"I've never tried most of those things, so I don't know if I'll actually like them, but they turn me on to think about or to watch, and I—" Shit. What was I doing? I was supposed to be encouraging him to want me, not telling him how unsure I was.

"That's why you need to explore with someone who knows what they're doing. When I'm with someone new to the scene, I take everything slowly, probably far slower than they want me to, and they can use their safeword anytime. It doesn't matter if it's my favorite thing—"

"What is your favorite thing?"

He shook his head. "I don't think—"

"Leo, I just had to tell you all the things I wanted to do, but I haven't gotten to see your list. I want to know what you like." I deliberately made my voice low and hopefully sexy.

He took a slow, deep breath. "Are you trying to kill me?"

I grinned. *Maybe a little.* "No, I just think it's fair for me to know something about you."

"Needle play; play piercing, to be more specific."

I sputtered and coughed a bit. "Really?" It was something I'd marked as a maybe, but it was a far-fetched maybe. I had been considered getting my nipples pierced, but I didn't expect it to turn me on.

"You asked."

"I did. I'm sorry. You just surprised me. I saw this video once where the Dom put thin needles all along his sub's cock. It was… wow."

Leo smiled. "I've done that."

My mouth dropped open as I stared at him. "D-do you want to do that to me?"

His face turned red. "Not for a while, and not if you don't want to."

I shivered. "Why does it sound so much hotter when you talk about it?"

He ran a hand over his hair. "Jesus, is it going to be like this all the time with you?"

"Like what?"

"Like you're trying to say anything and everything to get a reaction from me?"

I grinned. "Are you trying to say I don't have the submitting part down very well?"

He kept his expression very neutral. "It's something we could work on."

"I guess in my fantasies, I'm more of a pain slut than a submissive."

Leo made a sound like he might be choking.

"Is that wrong?"

He shook his head. "There is no wrong in this unless you're doing something without consent. But there is a level of surrender you have to be willing to offer if I'm going to find out where the limits of your pain tolerance are. It's perfectly normal to enjoy different aspects of submission, though. Trusting a man or woman with your body, trusting them to hurt you just enough for you to enjoy it, is a form of submission. It's different than being the type of submissive who wants to do whatever their Dom asks. Both are different from someone who primarily gets off on being an object for their Dom to play with. There are many varieties of D/s relationships."

"Wow. I guess there are."

He grinned. "There's no reason for you to have thought about anything beyond your own interests. Part of what we'll do is figure out exactly what you like and what you don't. If it turns out all you want is for someone you trust to hurt you in ways you find stimulating, then that's fine."

"But what do you want?" I was afraid he wouldn't answer, but I needed to know. I needed to see if I could be the right man for him.

"I want a man who gets off on receiving pain as much as I get off on giving it, who trusts me enough to let me push his limits, knowing I won't ever go past them. I want his submission, but only in that context."

I swallowed hard. That was exactly what I wanted or, at least, what I thought I wanted. "I can do that."

Leo arched a brow.

"I can *try* to do that."

He nodded. "Better. Trust is the most important part of this relationship, and it goes both ways. You must trust that I will stop if you use your safeword, and I have to trust that you will use it if you need to."

"I'll use it. I swear. I'm not going to let anyone do something I don't want."

"Good. And if you have a question or you need a break…?"

"I'll say yellow, and we'll talk about it." He gave me what seemed to be a reluctant smile, which told me that was the right answer. "Why are you so hesitant to be the one to explore with me?"

"I would be hesitant with anyone. I told you I don't work with new submissives much anymore."

"But surely you—"

"Will, I'm willing to try this, okay? But I need to lay out some ground rules."

I drew in a shaky breath before nodding. Trust was important to me too. I really should tell him who I was, but I couldn't ruin this, not now. Plenty of people in the BDSM scene went by nicknames or screen names, because they didn't want to be identified. It wasn't really a big deal. If I told myself that enough, maybe I'd believe it.

Avery hadn't thought it was wrong. Of course, he probably hadn't thought I was going to play with Leo. "Can these rules be altered later if they need to be?"

"Yes," Leo said. "At any point if either of us want to change something, we can discuss it."

"Okay, what are your rules?"

"I will work with you for three months. We can meet as frequently as our schedules allow during that time period. I'll help you explore some of the basic possibilities for pain play, so you can figure out what you like in a safe environment, and you'll be ready to ask future partners for what you want."

"Why the time limit?"

Leo closed his eyes and rubbed his forehead.

"Am I really that exasperating?"

He huffed. "I don't know. Maybe I'm just really old."

"You're not old." If there was one thing my dad's relationship with Avery had taught me, it was that age didn't matter.

"I'm way older than you."

I shrugged. "Why should that matter?"

"It shouldn't, as long as you're comfortable with it."

"I'm very comfortable with it. Like I said, if Avery trusts you, then I trust you. Not to mention you're hot as fuck, and I'm ready to get on my knees for you right now. I'm ready to feel your hands on me, to have you torment me."

He cleared his throat. "I... um... I get the idea. Will these terms work for you?"

"As long as there's the chance to extend things if we both want that."

He frowned as he considered my statement. "Three months will be plenty of time."

"What if it's not? We don't even live in the same town, or we won't unless I go to grad school. We might not be able to meet very often."

"We'll manage."

"But if we—"

He sighed. "We can discuss it after the three months are up."

"All right. Then I accept. Should we start now or set up a time to get together?"

"Now?" He shook his head. "Boy, you really are going to challenge me, aren't you?"

I shrugged. "I guess so."

"I want you to take some time to think about this and be sure it's what you want. I'll have a contract for you to sign when we get together again."

I tried not to pout, but I didn't think I succeeded. "I've been thinking about this for years, thinking about it and not doing anything about it. Then when I tried, it was—"

"Fucked up and wrong, and I'm really sorry you got hurt. I'm honored that you trust me, but I still want you to take a few days to think about it."

"Just a few days?"

He gave that exasperated sigh again. "Yes. Why don't we get together Sunday night? Will that work for you?"

"Yes! Here?"

"Here is good."

"Great." In three days, I would know if my fantasies were just as hot in reality as they were in my head. God, I hoped they would be. And I hoped Leo wouldn't regret deciding to be the one to introduce me to pain play, especially if—when?—he found out I was Graham's son.

4

LEO

I was running a few minutes late for our appointment, so I texted Will to let him know I would meet him by the bar. A patron had left their wallet on the bathroom sink, and no one had turned it in, so it had likely been stolen. It took me longer than I expected to reach a point where I could leave the matter to my security team and go meet Will, so by the time I headed to the bar, I was praying he didn't think I'd stood him up.

Fortunately, he was still there, leaning against the polished wooden bar, talking to Marie, one of my most reliable bartenders. I slowed my pace, giving myself a few moments to study Will. He was in all black. His jeans hugged his firm legs and made his ass look even more rounded than it had the last time I'd seen him. I wanted to hear him cry out as I struck those lush cheeks. I wanted to see them all red and welted.

I was not starting out the way I'd intended. I needed to be more objective than this if I was going to explore with him without letting myself get too involved. But his T-shirt clung to his muscular body, showing off his wide shoulders and those biceps that I was dying to lick. It was going to be hard to hold myself back tonight. But I would, because this wasn't about me. It was about Will having a chance to learn what he liked and what he didn't. I was his teacher, not his lover.

"Will!" I called. He didn't turn around, so I said his name again. Still no reaction. I waited until I was right beside him. "Hi, Will. Sorry I'm so late."

He turned around then, seeming startled. "Oh, you were calling *me*? I didn't recognize—I mean I… sorry."

His reaction seemed odd, but maybe he was just nervous. "I've got a private room for us if you're ready."

"Oh! Yes. I'm ready. And this is just ginger ale. I remembered the rule about no drinking during a scene."

I smiled. "Very good. Do you remember my other rules for tonight?"

"Use my safeword if I need it. Ask questions if I'm unsure. Never do anything I don't really want. What else?"

He was so fucking adorable and so eager to please. How had I thought I wouldn't end up wanting more with him? "We'll talk about that when we get to the room. Come on."

He followed me upstairs to the space I'd reserved for us. I unlocked the door and ushered him in. The room had a bed, a chair, a spanking bench, and a cabinet filled with toys and safe sex supplies.

When I turned to look at him, Will seemed more jittery than I'd seen him since the first night we talked.

"Are you doing okay?"

"Um… yeah…" He looked away and then back at me. "I'm just nervous."

"Which is very normal."

"Yeah. I guess so. How do we start? Do I just take my clothes off or what?"

I couldn't help but smile. He seemed so innocent, even if I knew he really wasn't. "We're going to talk for a few minutes first. I want you to know exactly what will happen, and I need to set some clear boundaries."

Will sat on the bed, so I took the chair, which worked well. He wasn't as likely to feel intimidated since he was looking down at me. "I know we talked about this a little, but have you explored kink at all in any way, even on your own?"

"Well, I've had a guy slap my ass a few times while he fucked me, but that doesn't really count. I've played around some myself with nipple clamps and hot wax and really big dildos."

Oh, fuck. The thought of watching him torment himself while I jerked off was nearly too much for me.

"I know it's kind of weird, but if I do something that hurts, it makes me come so much harder." His cheeks turned pink, and he looked away.

"Will, it's not weird at all. It's just how you're wired. When I do those things to other people, it makes me come harder. I know it's not easy to talk about these things, but communication between play partners is very important."

He nodded. "I know. I... I'm trying."

"You're doing a great job, bo—Do you mind if I call you boy?"

His eyes widened, and he sucked in his breath in a way that told me he didn't mind at all. "No... No, I... I like it."

"Good. Do you want to use red or something else for your safeword?"

"Red is good."

"And yellow to slow down or take a break?"

"Yes, Sir." He gave me a questioning look. "Should I call you Sir?"

"If you want to. We're just warming up to things today, so I won't expect it."

"Okay, Sir."

I smiled, loving that he wanted to use the honorific anyway.

"I will have you take your clothes off in a few moments, and if you're comfortable with it, I'll restrain you on the spanking bench. I'll use my hand to spank you first, and then I'll move on to a paddle. Any time you need to stop or slow down or talk about what's happening, use red or yellow. Do you understand?"

"Yes, Sir."

His soft acknowledgement of my dominance went straight to my cock, making me wish I weren't determined to lay out the rest of my ground rules. "I know you want this to be about sex as well as pain, but since this is our first time, I won't be touching you sexually."

"But I—"

I held up a hand. "I need to focus on your reactions today, but I will allow you to come."

"*Allow* me?" He raised his brows.

"Now there's the challenge I expected from you."

"But if I need to come, I just do."

"I expect my subs to learn to hold back their orgasm until I give them permission. Are you wiling to try that?"

"I… um… yes." I fought to keep from smiling at the determined look on his face.

"It might take you a while to learn, but you will."

He grinned. "You're so hot like that, all confident and in charge."

"That is kind of the idea here."

He shrugged. "I guess so."

"If you're ready, strip and position yourself over the

bench with your knees on the pads here." I pointed to the kneeling pads.

Will's hands shook as he gripped the hem of his T-shirt. Was he really okay? I hoped so.

He pulled it over his head and tossed it onto the chair in the corner of the room. His chest and abs were just as defined as I'd expected, his skin smooth and pale, and he had a smattering of trimmed dark chest hair. He was perfection, and I wanted to touch him everywhere.

When his hands went to the fastenings of his pants, he looked up at me. I nodded to encourage him, needing to swallow before I could speak. "Take them off, Will."

"Yes, Sir."

He pushed them over his hips, taking his briefs too, and his cock sprang free. He was fully hard, despite his obvious nerves. I wanted to wrap my hand around his shaft and feel its weight, the soft skin, and the hardness underneath. I also wanted to see how he'd react if I took him into my mouth. But I wasn't going to do any of those things today. I needed to move slowly. I could pretend that was for him, because he was new to this, but it was for me too. I was supposed to be teaching him about D/s and pain play. I had to remember that I was just his play partner, not his lover. The more I touched him, the more easily I might forget that.

When Will was fully naked, he looked at me again, holding my gaze. Something in those dark eyes sent a thrill through me. There was no denying the chemistry between us, but he was only twenty-two, and I was looking for something serious, something real and permanent. Surely he wasn't ready for that.

Avery was ready for that with Graham.

Avery was an exception, and he was older than Will.

"Leo? Sir?"

24

Fuck, I'd let my thoughts wander. I was the Dom. I was supposed to be in control, but I was already letting Will get to me. "I'm sorry."

"Are you alright?" I hated how worried he looked.

"I'm supposed to be the one asking that."

"Really? Damn, there are way too many rules to all this."

I rolled my eyes, and then we both laughed, breaking the tension.

Will turned toward the bench, showing me his gorgeous, round ass. I had to sink my nails into my palms not to get lost in fantasies again. What was wrong with me? I used to be so good at being detached enough to be a teacher while still giving a sub what they needed.

Maybe that's why you burned out on it.

I helped Will position himself, and every time I touched him, heat rushed through me. I was sure he could tell how hard I was. I'd have to hope he wouldn't mention it or push for me to fuck him. I wasn't sure I'd be able to hold out if he begged me.

"Are you comfortable?" I asked when I'd strapped his wrists and ankles in place.

"As much as I can be when I'm restrained and exposed like this."

I arched a brow at him, but he just smirked at me. Challenging indeed. He might enjoy saying "Sir" when he chose, but he was nothing like the naturally submissive young men I usually gravitated to. I'd thought I had a clear type. Apparently, my cock disagreed.

"Can you wiggle your fingers and toes?"

He nodded.

"Does anything hurt or feel tingly?"

"No, really, I'm fine."

I moved behind him. "You *are* quite exposed like this, aren't you?"

He shivered, and my cock grew even harder.

"I could do anything to your ass now. Do you realize that?"

"Yes, Sir." His voice was low and husky. He didn't sound the least bit scared.

"I want you to take some long, slow breaths."

He did as I said, and I laid my hand on his back, feeling it rise and fall, letting him get used to me touching him. I slid my hand up and down his back. Then I began to caress his ass.

"I'm going to spank you now. I'll go easy at first. Then I'll increase the force. After I've gotten you good and warmed up, I'll use the paddle on you, but I'll warn you first. Is that okay?"

"Yes, Sir."

I smiled, loving how easily the words came to him, despite his reluctance to surrender in other ways.

"What should you do if you need me to stop?"

"I'll say red, Sir."

"And if you tell me no or simply ask me to stop?"

"You'll keep going."

"That's right, boy. So feel free to protest all you want. If I think you may have forgotten your safeword, I'll check in with you and make sure I still have your consent."

"Thank you, Sir."

I squeezed his ass, digging my fingers in until he gasped. Then I let him go and brought my hand down across his ass.

The first blow made him jump. He wriggled as I gave him several more blows, but he didn't really fight, and he stayed nearly silent.

"You don't have to hold anything in," I said. "I love to hear my subs cry out, protest, beg."

He shook his head. I shouldn't have been surprised that he was going to make me work for his cries and whimpers. I'd get them, though. I always did.

I slapped his ass harder and kept the blows coming. He held his body taut, which would only make the pain worse. He was panting, but he still bit back all those delicious sounds I wanted to hear. It was going to be so fun to break him.

I went at him hard until his ass was bright red. I paused then and rubbed the heated skin. He gasped, but then he sank his teeth into his lip to prevent any more sounds from escaping. I could see his cock hanging heavy between his legs, precum glistening at the tip. I longed to wrap my hand around it, so I could feel how hard he was. I was impressed with his ability to take what I'd given him. Finding his limits was going to be intoxicating, but I wasn't going to go much further today. I didn't want him to regret what we'd done.

"I'm going to switch to a paddle now. Say green if you're okay with that."

"Green." The word was more a harsh exhale than true speech, which made me think he needed a short break.

"Before I give you more, I want you to take five deep breaths. When you exhale, imagine sinking into the bench. The more tense you are, the more this will hurt."

"Want it to hurt. Feels so good."

Holy fuck. If he knew what those words did to me… "I know, baby, but you should also feel relaxed afterwards."

I froze. I couldn't remember ever calling a man "baby" before.

WREN

Wow, he'd called me baby! I liked that. A lot. "I can't relax until I can come."

Leo chuckled. "I need to hear you scream before I let you come."

I shook my head. I couldn't do that. It felt too vulnerable somehow. I'd found the courage to ask Leo for this. He could see I was hard and needy from what he'd done to me, but letting him hear how it affected me was just... too much. And yet... I didn't want to use my safeword, because part of me needed him to pull those sounds from me anyway, to force me to give him what he'd asked for.

"Breathe, boy."

Fuck. I loved him calling me boy as much as baby. I drew in a shaky breath.

"Good. Now deeper and slower."

I tried to take some slow, steady breaths, but how could I relax when I was so fucking horny? My body buzzed from the spanking he'd given me.

I must have relaxed enough to please him, because he tapped the leather-covered paddle against my ass.

"Ready?"

I nodded. And he kept tapping me lightly, alternating from one side to the other. Then, without any warning, he brought the paddle down hard. Pain shot through me, making me writhe. I braced for more but nothing else came.

"I'll give you what you want when you loosen up," Leo said.

"I don't know how to do that, Sir." Tears stung my eyes. I didn't want to fucking cry any more than I wanted to scream or beg.

Leo stroked my back, soothing me with his touch.

Eventually, I was able to relax. He massaged my shoulders, and I felt like I was melting into the leather bench. He continued to work my stiff muscles, moving down my back. When he dug his fingers into my sore ass, I managed to breathe through it rather than tensing up again.

"Good boy."

Before I could respond, he smacked my ass with the paddle, and I bit my lip, barely holding in my cry. He was going to fucking break me. And dear God, I wanted him to.

"I want to hear you, boy. I want you to give me everything you're holding inside."

Crack! Fuck, the paddle hurt so bad.

Another blow. I fought the restraints, but I still didn't make a sound. Why couldn't I just let go and give him what he wanted? Why was I so fucking stubborn?

"Boy, I know this hurts. I want to hear it."

"No. I can't. I... no!"

Leo squeezed my aching ass, and I whimpered, hating that he'd pulled even that small sound from me. "Boy, I need to check in with you. I want to make sure you remember how to stop me."

"I say red, Sir." But I wasn't going to, not even if he pushed. He could force me to scream for him. I wanted him to. I needed him to.

"Good. Now give me what I want." He hit me again and again. Pain threatened to overtake me. I needed relief. I needed to come. I needed to scream. Finally, I gave in, crying out Leo's name, whining, begging. It all felt so good.

"Beautiful, boy. So beautiful. You can come now." He released my hands, and I reached between my legs, too tired to sit up. I worked my cock in hard, fast strokes, and in seconds, my climax raced through me, lighting me up. My body shook as my cum shot from my dick.

5

LEO

I was afraid I'd gone too far. I shouldn't have pushed a novice as far as I had pushed Will. But he'd been so beautiful, so full of pent-up need. And if I were honest, I'd been just as needy. No scene had felt this right to me in ages. I wouldn't have been shocked if my cock had busted right through my zipper as Will came. I wanted to open my pants and jerk off until my cum decorated his back. I was almost certain he'd welcome it, but I'd made a promise to myself, and I was sticking to it.

I knelt beside him and stroked his back. "That was so good, boy. You gave me everything I asked for. Are you okay now?"

"Yes, Sir." His voice was soft, and he looked completely blissed out. All the tension that had ridden him before was gone. He stayed slumped over the bench as I uncuffed his ankles. Then I helped him up and practically carried him to the bed.

He mumbled something that sounded like "thank you" as I positioned him on his side and pulled a blanket over him. I knew he'd get cold quickly as he came back from subspace.

"I'm going to get you some water and some chocolate, but I won't leave the room. Stay right there, okay?" His eyes fluttered open, and he smiled at me. I fought the urge to lean down and kiss him. Just a soft brush of my lips against his forehead to give him some comfort could be considered aftercare, not something sexual, but it would still cross the line I'd drawn for myself.

I crossed the room and grabbed water from the mini fridge and a chocolate bar from a shelf in the cabinet. When I returned to Will, I opened the water and held it to his lips, not sure he was capable of holding the bottle himself yet. He took a few swallows, and when I pulled it away, he smiled. "Thank you, Sir."

"You're welcome. Here." I handed him the chocolate. "Your blood sugar is probably low after all that. I asked a lot of you."

"You gave me exactly what I wanted."

"I did?"

He nodded, rising up until he was propped on his elbow. "Tonight was everything I hoped for."

My breath caught, and I allowed myself to push his sweaty curls back from his face. "I'm glad."

"I want you to do more to me, and I want you to fuck me next time, after you make me beg for it. I think I like surrendering more than I thought I would. I just need to be pushed to do it."

He still sounded a bit out of it, and I had no doubt he was still floating, not yet back to the real world. I couldn't take what he said too seriously, certainly not until we had a chance to talk when we weren't in scene space, but that didn't stop me from hoping he truly meant it. "We'll decide our next step later. Right now, you need to rest."

"Will you rest with me? You can hold me, right? It's not sex if you just lay with me."

"I don't know if—"

"Please. I'm cold. So cold." Tears spilled over and ran down his cheeks.

Without any more hesitation, I climbed on the bed and pulled him into my arms. "It's okay, baby. That's just all the emotions we brought up in our scene." He clung to me as he sobbed, seeming to need an anchor. "I've got you. I won't let you go."

Several moments later, the tears slowed and then stopped. He pulled away and looked at me, and the intensity of what I saw in his eyes nearly knocked me over. There was hope and longing there, but also fear. I wasn't sure what to say to him, so I just pulled him to me for another hug. "Are you feeling better?"

He nodded against my shoulder. "I think I'm okay now."

He shifted like he was going to get off the bed, but I stopped him with a hand on his shoulder. "Don't try to stand yet. It takes a while to come down from a scene like this."

He nodded. "I do still feel kind of dizzy, but the spanking felt so good. And I don't know why I cried. I liked it. I really did."

"A lot of subs cry after a scene. Like I said before, there are a lot of emotions that get stirred up. It doesn't mean you aren't happy, just that you need to process all that's happened."

He smiled, still looking a little punch-drunk. "You're so good to me."

"I want to give you what you need. You deserve to be taken care of."

"How soon can we do this again?"

It warmed me all over that he wanted more. "You're going to need to wait a while for your ass to heal."

He winced as he shifted on the bed. "I didn't realize how sore I was until a few minutes ago."

"Roll over on your stomach. I've got some ointment that will help you heal faster. You'll be fine in a few days. I promise."

"So we can meet again in a few days?"

God, that was tempting. "No. We should wait until next weekend."

"I have to go a whole week?" He looked devastated.

"Yes, you do." I was usually good at staying firm, but I was dying to give in to him and say I'd meet him as soon as he wanted to.

"You're absolutely sure I can't suck you off to thank you?" He smiled coyly, and damn if I didn't want his pouty lips wrapped around my cock.

"No. We'll renegotiate sexual contact when we're not coming down from a scene."

He huffed. "You're so fucking responsible."

"Please don't consider playing with anyone who's not."

He shook his head. "I wouldn't. I'm teasing. I like how responsible you are, because you make me feel safe. That's why I don't want to play with anyone else."

His words made me shiver. I hadn't truly wanted to play with anyone in a long time, and I knew there was no way I could play with him again and not touch him sexually. I was going to give in to him. I just hoped I wouldn't wind up brokenhearted when this ended.

WREN

I'D FINALLY GOTTEN steady enough on my feet to get dressed. When I was ready to go, Leo said, "Would next Sunday at the same time work for you?"

I started to say yes, but I kept hearing his words about the importance of trust over and over in my mind. He'd given me exactly what I wanted, making sure I was okay at every step along the way. And in return, I'd hidden something from him, something he deserved to know.

Before I could thoroughly think through the consequences, words flew from my mouth. "Will isn't really my name. It's Wren, and I'm Graham's son."

Leo just stared at me, mouth open. I'd expected anger. But seconds passed, and he said absolutely nothing. I started to shake again and had to sit down.

"I'm sorry. I should've told you to start with."

"I'm assuming Avery knew that night when he called me, but he didn't tell me either."

Shit. I didn't want him blaming Avery for this. "I wouldn't let him call unless he promised not to give you my name, because I didn't want my dad to know what happened. He thought you'd counsel me. He couldn't have known that we'd feel like this about each other."

Leo frowned. "I would never have told your dad something you told me in confidence like that. You needed help, and I would've given it no matter who you were."

"I know that now. I… Fuck. I'm sorry. I still want this. I still want you, but I had to tell you the truth."

Leo was shaking his head. And I knew he was going to reject me. Why the fuck had I decided to be honest now?

"I knew you looked familiar, but I couldn't figure out why. I just assumed I'd seen you in Thrust or something, but now I know it's because I've seen pictures of you as a kid."

The last thing I wanted was him thinking of me as a child. "I'm an adult now. What we're doing isn't wrong."

Leo took a slow breath before he said anything else. I waited, trying not to get my hopes up that he'd see reason but doing it anyway. "Objectively, you're right. We're both adults. We both consented, and there's nothing wrong with what we just did, but I can't see you again."

"Please, don't—"

"I won't hide this from Graham, and telling him would fuck up our friendship. He's too important to me to risk that."

I knew they had years of history and that Leo had helped my dad after Dad had come out and my mom had sent him packing, but having Leo so easily choose my dad over me still hurt. "I guess I've ruined everything."

Leo shook his head. "I would've eventually figured it out. I really appreciate you telling me before this went any further. I just wish you'd told me to start with."

I didn't, because at least I'd had this one evening with him. "Look. I know you're angry."

"Yes, I am." He brushed a hand over his short hair. "I still can't quite believe I just spanked my best friend's son."

"I know it's weird for you, but Leo, please, I think we could make this work."

He shook his head. "No. It's just not… I can't. I'll be thinking about other Doms you'd be compatible with. You need to explore more, but it can't be with me."

"This isn't fair. I'm not a child." Even if that pouty outburst made me sound like one.

"No, you're not. If I thought you were, I would never have agreed to this."

Leo could give me a list of names if that made him feel better, but I doubted I'd contact anyone. I didn't want someone else, I wanted him. Tears stung my eyes. I was absolutely not going to cry again before I got out of there. I turned toward the door and reached for the knob.

"Wren?"

Hearing my real name made me freeze. What would it have been like if he'd called me that as he'd spanked me?

"Yes?" I didn't turn around. I wasn't ready to face him again.

"I do appreciate you telling me. That took a lot of courage."

"But it didn't make you respect me enough to see me again."

"It's not about me respecting you. It's about my friendship with Graham."

"He doesn't have any right to be angry with you. He's dating a man twenty years younger than him. He even... I guess you know the kinds of things he likes. I'm okay with the two of them, so why shouldn't he have to accept whatever I want to do?"

Leo sighed. "He should accept any consensual thing you do, but I can't be the one to do it with you."

Hot anger rushed through me. "If I were older, if—"

"If you were older, this whole situation would be different. You're an adult, but you're also his son."

I bit my lip hard, forcing myself to hold back the tears that threatened to fall. I had to get out of there before I let myself cry over this stubborn asshole. "You can send me names of other Doms if you want to, but you're the one I want."

I walked away then, not wanting to hear any more reasons why we shouldn't be together, no matter how logical they were.

6

LEO

My phone rang. I glanced at the screen and saw it was Marie calling. She was working the bar tonight, so something must be up.

"It's Leo."

"Hey. I've got a young guy here at the bar. He's had a lot to drink. A couple guys have gotten a bit aggressive with him. He held his own with them, but he really needs to go home, and he's not listening to me."

"Is he behaving dangerously?"

"No, he's just wasted and babbling about how he's had the worst week ever."

I sighed. It wasn't even eleven yet, but it had already been a long night. I could send one of my security officers to deal with this, but I hated for them to leave their stations if this guy only needed a nudge to head home. "I'll be there in a minute."

I yawned as I pulled my office door closed. I hadn't slept well for the last few nights, and when I did sleep, I dreamed of Wren, of touching him, flogging him, trying out everything on his list. Thinking about him all the time was driving me crazy.

I hadn't told anyone what had happened between the two of us, and I assumed Wren hadn't either, but I was still scared Graham would find out somehow. I'd pondered just confessing, but I couldn't do that without talking to Wren. And if I saw Wren, I wasn't sure I could keep from giving in to what he wanted. I'd just had to pray Graham didn't find out.

At least encouraging a drunk kid to go home would distract me for a while.

Or so I thought.

When I reached the bar, the young man turned out to be Wren.

I almost walked away and called security after all. Sure, Wren might be pissed and a bit scared to have a uniformed officer approach him. But they were good at their jobs. They'd coax him out of the bar and put him in a cab. The problem was, I couldn't be sure where he'd go then. Fuck. I owed it to Graham to make sure Wren got home safely, which meant I'd be the one taking him home.

I had a good crew working that night. They'd be fine on their own until closing. I would take Wren home and put him to bed. Alone. Very much alone.

Then tomorrow I would call him, and we would have a serious talk. I had to make him understand that we were truly done.

Marie caught my eye as I approached the bar. When she inclined her head toward Wren, I signaled to let her know I understood.

"Wren, what's up?"

He turned toward me. His eyes widened and then he smiled. "Leo. You're here. I came to your club. I wanted to see what it was all about, but then I tried this drink and it

was good, so I had another one and another and then…"
He looked at Marie and held up a glass filled with a pink
and no doubt potent concoction. "How many have I had?"

"More than enough," I said, taking the glass from him
and giving it to Marie.

"No. I need one more. You can have one with me. We
can all have one," he said, looking at Marie.

The bartender shook her head. "No drinking while I'm
on the job."

"I've got this," I assured her, and she headed toward
the other end of the bar where a few customers were
waiting.

I turned back to Wren. "It's time you headed home."

"You kicking me out?"

"No, I'm taking you home."

He shook his head. "I want another drink first."

"No more drinks. You need to go to bed."

He grinned. "With you? That's even better than
a drink."

"Alone. To sleep this off."

I took his arm and encouraged him to slide off his
stool. He would've sunk to the ground if I hadn't held onto
him. Marie glanced over and moved our way again. "He's
a friend. I'm going to take him home. I'll let security know
I'm heading out, but give me a call if there are any
problems."

"All right. Have a good night, boss."

Wren leaned against me as we walked to my truck. I
tried not to think about how good he felt as I wrapped my
arm around his waist to support him.

"Did you drive here?" I asked.

"Nope. Took an Uber. An Uuuu-ber. That's such a
funny word." He started laughing so hard he almost made
us both fall down. This was going to be a long drive.

"Where do you live?" I asked when I had him settled in my car.

"Are you really putting me to bed, Leo? You could spank me again, you know? You could even make me beg for it."

Thank God he was drunk. While I wanted him, I would never do a scene when he couldn't consent. If he'd been sober, I might not have been able to say no. "There isn't going to be any spanking. I'm going to take you home, get you some water and ibuprofen, tuck you in bed, and call you tomorrow."

"You never called me. You said you would, but you didn't."

He had me there. I was supposed to call him with names of other Doms he could trust to help him, but I hadn't, because I didn't want to think about him with anyone else. Ugh. I was so fucked. "I'm sorry. I should have—"

A snore alerted me to the fact that Wren wasn't listening, and he also wasn't going to tell me his address. I'd just take him to the condo I stayed at while I was in Asheville working at Thrust. I could drop him off at his apartment in the morning.

I only managed to get him half awake when we arrived. At least my guest room was on the first floor.

I unlocked his door and managed to half carry, half drag him to bed. I tried to get him to drink some water, but he was too out of it. So I just took off his shoes and pants and rolled him over on his side. Damn, he was hot, lying there in briefs and a T-shirt with his curly hair all mussed. If he were sober...

I left the glass of water on the nightstand along with a bottle of ibuprofen. I was headed upstairs to my bedroom when I heard him cry out in anguish. I raced into his room, heart pounding. He didn't seem to be awake, but he was mumbling and twisting on the bed like he was fighting someone or something.

"No! Stop it! No!" he shouted.

"Wren! It's okay. I'm here."

"Leo? Leo, save me."

I pulled him into my arms. "I'm here. I've got you."

After a few minutes, he quieted down and fell back into a sound sleep without ever fully waking. Had he been dreaming about being attacked? I began to reconsider tracking down the asshole who'd hurt Wren and teaching him about fear.

I eased off the bed, but I didn't want to leave him in case he had another nightmare. If I stayed on the couch in the living room, I'd be able to hear him if he called out. I'd fallen asleep on it watching TV several times and not been the worse for wear. I grabbed an extra pillow and a blanket from the hall closet and settled in, refusing to let myself think too hard about how protective he made me feel.

7

WREN

I felt like something was trying to claw its way out from inside my head. I moaned and curled into a ball. Was I dying?

"Wren?"

That sounded like Leo. Great. Something—An alien? A Greek goddess? A mutant spider?—was pushing through my skull, and now I was hearing voices. I shifted positions, trying to ease the pain. My stomach lurched, letting me know it was about to expel its contents, possibly along with most of my internal organs. A trash can appeared in front of me, and I was suddenly too busy vomiting to wonder where it came from. I had to be dying. Or maybe I'd already died, and I was in hell.

A hand rubbed my back. "It's okay. I'm here."

Leo? He couldn't be here, could he? If he was, I wasn't dead. Leo wouldn't be in hell. He'd only be with me if I were in heaven.

My stomach finally calmed. I wiped my mouth with the back of my hand and slumped onto my bed. "I'm dying, aren't I?"

Leo—or hallucination Leo—chuckled. "I'm not surprised you feel like that. You were so drunk I could barely get you into the condo."

Drunk? Was I drunk? No, not anymore. I was hung over as fuck, so I must have been drunk last night. I'd gone to Leo's club and... What the hell was he doing here?

I forced my eyes to open so I could look at him. He seemed real enough. "Are you a hall-hallu... Are you real?"

He frowned. "Yes. Are you okay?"

"No." I remembered in time that shaking my head was a very bad idea.

"Alright. That was a stupid question. But I don't need to take you to the hospital or anything, do I?"

"No, I'm just dying."

"Right. Any chance you could keep some water down?"

Water. Could I drink water? My stomach clenched in response to that thought. "I don't think so."

"All right, but I don't want you to get dehydrated. You'll have to at least have some ice chips soon."

Now Hallucination Leo was using his teacher voice.

"Later." I closed my eyes again, but I sensed Leo still there beside my bed. "Are you going to watch me sleep?"

"Do you remember last night?" Apparently he was ignoring my question.

"A little. The bartender told me I couldn't have any more. She told me I should go home, and then... you came to make me leave."

"I did. Marie called me, but I didn't know it was you until I got to the bar."

"So you wouldn't have taken just anybody home?"

He sighed. "No."

"But you're still here. You are, aren't you? I really hope

this isn't all a hallucination." Huh. I was able to say the word this time.

"Of course I'm still here. This is my condo."

I smiled, and just that small movement hurt my head. "You rescued me and brought me to home?"

"I did."

"You like to rescue me."

He huffed. "I like helping people. You needed help last night."

Remembering to move very slowly, I managed to sit up. I grimaced when I got a whiff of my own scent. "I should shower. And brush my teeth and…"

"Drink some water."

I might be able to handle a few sips, but water wasn't what I wanted. "I need coffee."

"If you think you can manage showering by yourself, I'll make coffee, but you have to promise me you'll drink some water first."

"Are you volunteering to shower with me?"

He scowled. "I'm trying to keep you from falling down and cracking your skull on the tile."

"I'll be fine," I grumbled.

"Then coffee and water will be waiting for you."

"You'll still be here when I get out of the shower, right? You don't, like, have to go to work or anything? I want to apologize when I can think a little more clearly."

He nodded. "I'll be here."

I was able to stand without vomiting again, but my stomach churned, letting me know it didn't approve of my being upright. I picked up the wastebasket and carried it with me to the bathroom. I was horrified enough that Leo had seen me puke. I would die if he tried to clean up after me.

Once I'd washed the drunken night off myself and my

mouth no longer tasted like a skunk had died in it, I put on sleep pants and a T-shirt and followed the smell of coffee to the kitchen. I felt a bit more steady now, but I needed caffeine to ease the pounding in my head. I tried to move past Leo to get to the coffee pot, but he pointed to the glass of water on the counter. "Water first."

"I drank some in the bathroom."

He wouldn't relent, so I drank about half the glass, the sips going down easier than my earlier ones. "Do I get coffee now?"

Instead of answering, Leo filled a mug and handed it to me. I breathed in the steam before drinking it. It smelled damn good, which likely meant I'd be able to keep it down.

After I took several sips, I set it on the counter and looked at Leo. He was watching me intently.

My stomach started to roil again, but this time I was sure it was all from nerves. While I couldn't remember everything I'd said, I was sure I'd been an asshole the night before. What had I been thinking, going to Thrust?

"I was wrong to come looking for you at your club. I'm sorry. Thank you for not letting me do something even stupider."

Leo stepped closer, and my body reacted to his proximity. "Apology accepted. Right now might not be the best time, but we do need to talk more about this."

Was there a chance he'd reconsider being my Dom? Probably not, but if so, I wanted to be at my best when we talked about it. I was still nauseous and a bit dizzy. My headache had dulled, but it was still there. I wasn't ready to talk.

"I guess you're right, but…" I didn't want to leave. It seemed ridiculous, but I hated the idea of spending the morning at home alone. I was having trouble shaking off the bad dreams I'd had the night before.

"Wren, what is it?"

"Could I stay for a little longer? I… I just don't want to be alone."

"What's wrong? Is it whatever woke you up last night?" Shit, he'd heard me. Did that mean he really had come to comfort me? I'd thought that was part of the dream.

"Yes… I… I keep thinking about it."

"Are you having nightmares about the guy who assaulted you?"

I didn't want to admit that to Leo. I knew he already worried that I only wanted him because he'd been the one to help me afterward. Avery had rescued me initially, though, and I didn't want to fuck him. "Yes, but—"

Leo held up his hand, silencing me. "You don't have to explain. You can stay."

"Can we just watch a movie or something? You're right about now not being a good time for a serious talk."

"How about you pick out a movie?" He gestured toward the TV in his living room. "And I'll see about making us some breakfast?"

"That's perfect. Do you have bacon? I feel like lots of bacon."

He chuckled. "I do. I'll have a greasy hangover-cure breakfast ready soon."

8

LEO

Wren started to drift off about halfway through the movie. I put my arm around him and pulled him to me, so he could rest his head on my shoulder. Once he was fully asleep, he snuggled into me, all warm and relaxed. He felt so good. My more practical side said I should lay him down, cover him with a blanket, and walk away. But he'd told me he didn't want to be alone, so I wasn't going to leave him.

The movie was long over, and I was reading a book on my phone, when Wren finally woke. He blinked a few times and then looked up at me, giving me a soft smile. He watched me with such intensity and wonder that I gave in to what I wanted and kissed him.

I meant it to be a sweet kiss, one that spoke of comfort and love, but when Wren wrapped his arms around my neck and pulled me to him, the kiss grew fiercer. We both let out all the pent-up need we'd been feeling. Before I could tell myself no, I was tugging him over my lap. He straddled me, and our bodies pressed together as we devoured each other's mouths. His hard length rubbed against mine, and I gripped his ass, pulling him tighter against me.

He pressed his palm against my hard cock. I knew I should stop this, but when he started sliding his hand up and down, I forgot why.

"Want you," he murmured.

I unfastened his pants and pulled his cock out. Then I freed my own erection and took both of us in my hand. Wren groaned and thrust against me, trying to get more friction.

"I'm in control here," I growled.

"Fuck, yes. Please."

I kissed his neck, using my free hand to pull his T-shirt down so I could nibble along his collarbone. He worked his hips as I stroked both our shafts. I wanted to be inside him so badly. Just this once. That would be okay, wouldn't it? I'd already spanked him. "Wren, I know we haven't talked, and—"

He pressed a finger against my lips. "Please just give me this."

I gripped his waist and tried to lift him off, but he struggled. "Please don't make me stop."

"I'm not, but we need to change positions if I'm going to fuck you."

His eyes widened. "If you're... You are...? Oh God, yes, please."

I smiled at him, loving how flustered he was. "Finish undressing, then turn around and brace yourself over the back of the couch."

"Condoms? Lube?" he asked breathlessly as he threw his clothes off and positioned himself.

"Be right back." Walking to the bathroom gave me too much time to think. I imagined Graham's reaction to what we were about to do. I really didn't want to lose his friendship, but there was something about Wren that called to me. This wasn't just a hookup. It was so much more. Hadn't Graham told me he knew immediately with Avery? Was this meant to be too, me and Wren?

I would never have gone after him intentionally, but this… it just felt so right.

I was justifying what I wanted. I knew that, but I pushed away the nagging voice that said I should stop and grabbed the supplies we needed. When I stepped back into the living room, Wren had his arms folded along the back of the couch, and he was resting his head on them. His ass was tilted up, waiting for me. Fuck, I needed to be inside him. I flicked open the lube and slicked up a few fingers.

He groaned when I drew them along his crack and teased his hole. "Don't need prep. I just… need your cock."

God, I loved how eager he was. "I don't want to hurt you."

He laughed. "Seriously?"

"Dammit, I don't want to hurt you unintentionally."

"I don't think—"

I pushed two fingers into him, and he squirmed, pushing back, trying to get more. I worked him slowly, sliding in and out, determined to open him up enough that I could go hard once I buried my cock in him.

When I curled my fingers and pressed on his sweet spot, he cried out. "Now. Please. Need your cock."

"You'll get it when I'm ready."

He whined, no longer seeming to mind letting me hear the amazing sounds he could make. He was so fucking beautiful like this, all naked and needy. I reached underneath him and teased one of his nipples. When I pinched it hard, he cried out and drove himself back onto my fingers. I pinched harder, twisting the tight bud until he was panting and squirming, begging me to take him.

I couldn't wait any longer either. I pulled my fingers from his ass, and, not wanting to take the time to undress, I rolled on the condom and added lube as fast as I could. Wren arched his back deeply as I teased his hole with the tip of my cock. I pushed in slowly, not stopping until he'd taken all of me.

"God, you're tight," I whispered against the back of his neck as I kissed him. He wriggled, trying to work himself on me, and I slapped his ass. "I set the pace. You don't move until I say you can."

I held myself still for several seconds. I could see the muscles in his back straining as he struggled to keep himself still. I toyed with his nipples again, rolling them between my thumbs and forefingers. He whimpered, but he didn't move.

"You're doing such a good job of waiting for me, boy."

I reached down and fondled his balls, tugging on them gently. Then I ran my finger along his stretched rim.

"Oh, God. Please. Can't wait." He worked his hips, and I slapped his ass again, harder this time. "I told you not to move."

"I know, but I… Please, fuck me, Leo."

Something about him saying my name like that, in that desperate tone, took all my self-control. I pulled out and drove into him, rocking the couch and making him cry out. He pushed back, meeting my strokes as I fucked him.

"That's right, baby, fuck yourself on me. Show me how much you want my cock."

I slammed into him faster and faster. I worried we might tip the couch over, but I couldn't stop. He reached under himself, but I grabbed his wrist and returned his hand to the back of the couch. "Keep your hands right there."

"But I'm... I need—"

I slapped his ass hard enough to make him grunt. "No. I want to see if you can come hands-free."

"But I've never... I don't..." His words became mere sounds, and I didn't try to decipher them; I was too busy watching the way his ass bounced as I drove into him. I wasn't going to last much longer, no matter how much I wanted to. His tight channel felt too good.

"Are you ready to come, boy?"

"Yes. Please."

"I know you can do this for me. You can come without touching your cock."

"I don't—"

"It's what I want, and you want to please me, don't you?"

"Yes, God, yes."

I took hold of his hips, angling him so it was easier for my cock to hit his prostate. "Fuck. Leo. That's..."

"Come for me, baby."

"Yes, want to come, want..." I dragged my nails down his back, scratching him. He cried out and worked himself against me even harder.

I reached under him and pinched the same nipple I'd tormented before. That jolt of pain was all he needed. His ass squeezed me as he cried out his release, working his hips in jerky motions.

Hearing and seeing him giving himself over to his climax was too much for me. I thrust a few more times, and then I was coming too.

As I came down from the high of orgasm, all the reasons why Wren and I shouldn't have done this came flooding back. I pulled out and stumbled to the bathroom, head spinning as I tossed the condom and cleaned myself. What the hell had I been thinking? Nothing, that was what. I hadn't thought at all; I'd just acted on instinct, on lust. And oh, God, I'd just fucked Wren in the condo his father was letting me use.

How did Wren manage to wreck my self-control so easily? I'd bargained with myself, saying this could only happen one time, but it should never have happened at all. I'd told him no, and now I'd gone back on my word. Walking away again was going to hurt him more. It was going to hurt me too, but I deserved it. I should have stopped this, and I didn't.

The worst of it was, I already wanted him again. He was fucking perfect, the way he'd come hands-free when he thought he couldn't. The way hurting him had pushed him over the edge. But he was still my best friend's son. It didn't matter that he was an adult. It didn't matter that he'd wanted this as much as I had. Graham would still feel betrayed, and Wren was still so young, too young for all the things I wanted, the harsher and the softer ones.

I splashed cold water on my face, wet a washcloth for Wren, and braced myself for what I needed to do.

He was still lying over the back of the couch. He'd hardly moved except for sitting back on his heels. When I got close, he turned to look at me, and his eyes told me he knew I was going to say something he didn't want to hear.

"Wren—"

He held up a hand. "Don't say it."

"How do you know what I'm going to say?"

He glared at me. "Tell me I'm wrong."

God, how I wanted to. "I wish I could."

"Do you? Because if so, what's stopping you? I wish for a lot of things too. I'd like to know how it feels for you to use clamps on me instead of just your fingers. I'd like to know what it feels like when your flogger kisses my ass. I'd like to try things I'd never considered before meeting you, like electricity play or needle play. I'm up for all of it, Leo. You're the one who's preventing it."

My body wanted to tell him we could do all those things. I was afraid my heart did too, but I couldn't do it. "I'm sorry. I made a mistake, and—"

"No!" The force of his anger had me taking a step back. "It was not a mistake. I knew you'd say that. What just happened between us was amazing, and you know it. Are you really just going to dismiss me because I'm young and you think I don't know what I want?"

"That's not why—"

"I know you don't want to screw up your relationship with my dad. I don't either, but while it's fucking complicated, if you wanted to, we could figure it out."

"Wren, please, I—"

He pushed past me, picking up his clothes. "I don't want to hear any more. I'm going to get dressed, take some ibuprofen, and go home."

With tears blurring my vision, I scribbled a note which included the names of a few Doms Wren would be compatible with. I'd hurt him enough. I had no right to keep him from finding out more about what he enjoyed.

I set the note on the counter next to a fresh glass of water and the ibuprofen. Then I went upstairs where he wouldn't see me cry.

9

WREN

I was at my dad and Avery's new house, hiding upstairs, attempting to put together a shelf for their bedroom. They'd invited me to their housewarming party, and I knew they'd be hurt if I didn't attend, but Leo was going to be there, and I was not ready to see him. So I'd found a way to be helpful without having to mingle. I'd already tried to put the shelf together twice. Each time, I'd ended up with a few boards that weren't turned the right way. If I'd been in a hurry, I would've been furious. As it was, I didn't care if it took me all day.

I hadn't spoken to Leo since I'd scurried away from his condo. For the first few days, I'd foolishly hoped he'd call, saying he'd changed his mind. But no. Nothing. I hadn't gotten a chance to tell him I'd decided to accept my position in the master's program. I'd moved to Charlotte a week ago, and so far, the program seemed perfect for me, which was damn good, considering part of my motivation to accept was so I could be close to a man I wasn't even speaking to now.

"Wren?"

Shit, Avery was calling me. I was probably going to have to go downstairs.

"I'm still working on this damn shelf."

I heard footsteps on the stairs, and he appeared in the doorway. "Felicity's here, and she has jobs for everyone."

I groaned. "Seriously?"

"Oh, yes."

My sister-in-law was a force of nature. If she wanted me downstairs and I didn't go, she'd just come drag me there. I put down the useless instructions I'd been studying and followed Avery downstairs.

Everyone had gathered in the room at the front of the house that my dad intended to use as a music room once his piano was moved from Charlotte. My sister Mandy motioned for me to come stand by her.

"Are you all right?" she asked.

Did my nerves show that badly? "I'm fine, just frustrated with a stupid-ass shelf and its little picture directions."

She started to say something else, but Felicity called for everyone to be quiet. I only half-listened as Felicity organized all of us. Then I made the mistake of letting myself look at Leo. He was as gorgeous as ever, and my stupid cock still wanted him as badly as it had the first time I'd seen him. Leo looked up and our eyes met.

My heart began to trip over itself. I couldn't breathe. The edges of the room darkened. Fuck. I had to get out of there. I turned, nearly falling over a small table. Once I'd righted it, I rushed out of the room, hoping I hadn't given myself away to everyone.

After lunch was organized, most people went out back, so I decided to sit on the front porch where I wouldn't risk making eye contact with Leo again. After I'd been there a while, Avery's roommate, Sean, joined me. I warned him I wasn't good company, and encouraged him to go around back.

Then, as if to taunt me, Leo's deep voice echoed around the side of the house. The sound took me right back to that day I'd knelt on his couch as he pushed inside me. I still couldn't believe he'd made me come without touching myself. I hated how just hearing his voice made me want him so badly.

"I'm not feeling too celebratory either," Sean said as he perched on the porch railing. His words jolted me back to the present. "I'm happy for Avery and Graham, but I'm feeling kind of mixed up right now."

I sighed. "Yeah, me too."

"School shit?"

"No, school's great, actually. I… God, it sounds so stupid."

"What does?" Sean asked as I adjusted my position. I'd been befriended by a neighborhood cat, and she'd decided to start kneading my lap.

"You really don't have to listen to this."

"If I go out there," Sean tilted his head toward the back of the house, "I'm going to have to face some of my own shit. Trust me, I'm happy to listen."

Felicity had told me a bit about Sean's situation when she'd asked if I knew anyone looking for a roommate. Sean needed one now that Avery had moved out, but Avery and I both thought Sean really wanted to live with his boyfriend. "If facing your own shit means asking Blake if you can move in with him, then you better do it."

"Jesus, even you know about that?"

"Felicity's my sister-in-law. There's not much I don't know."

He huffed. "Fine, you already know my secret, so tell me yours."

I wasn't going to tell him everything, but I might as well explain the basics. "I decided to start this architecture program at the last minute, because there's a man I like who lives in Charlotte."

"And?"

"It's a good thing I'm loving school, because the thing with the guy is going nowhere."

"Yeah? That sucks."

I sighed. "He's older, and he thinks I'm not right for him, and I get why, but I just don't care. I want him anyway."

Sean got an odd look on his face that I couldn't read. He glanced toward the screen door and then out into the yard. When he finally looked at me again, he said, "Wren, I think I know who the man is."

My heart started to pound. "What? How?"

"When you fell over the table earlier, I saw who you were looking at."

"Oh, fuck!" The cat jumped off my lap and ran. I wanted to run too, but Sean sat down beside me on the porch swing and laid a hand on my arm.

"I don't think anyone else noticed, except maybe Mandy. Graham and Avery were too caught up in each other and their excitement about the house."

Even if my dad hadn't noticed, I needed to get out of there. I couldn't risk having to see Leo again. If I gave us away... "I should go. I didn't want to come, knowing he'd be here, but I didn't know how to say no when it was so important to my dad."

Sean got that same look on his face, and this time, I understood it as uncertainty. I was about to tell him to just say whatever was on his mind when he finally spoke. "You do know about the kinky stuff Leo likes, right?"

I pushed away my annoyance at the question. I knew

he meant well. "I might be the baby of the family, but I'm not as naive as some people think I am."

"I don't think you're naive or too young or anything else. I just wanted to check."

I sighed. Was there anyone who thought I deserved the relationship I wanted? "You probably still think he was right to reject me."

"I'm not sure there's a clear right or wrong for the two of you, but I get why he's skittish."

Skittish? Colts were skittish. Leo was… "I don't know that I'd use that word for him."

"No?"

"He's so fucking sure of himself."

Sean frowned. "From what Blake and Graham have said, Leo's not been himself for weeks. He's fucked up over this too."

Was that true? Was he really as affected by this as I was? *Don't get your hopes up.* "I get why he said we can't keep seeing each other, but I can't stop wanting him."

"*Keep* seeing each other?"

"We… um… saw each other a few times." We did a hell of a lot more than that, but I didn't need to get into TMI territory.

Sean grinned. "Is he as hot as I think he would be?"

"Hotter."

"Holy fuck."

"Sean? Are you in here?" Through the open window, I could see Blake looking into the music room.

"I'm on the porch," Sean called, then he glanced at me and whispered, "I won't say anything."

"Thank you," I said, keeping my voice equally low.

Blake pushed the screen door open and stepped onto the porch. "What are you two doing out here? We're ready to eat."

"Wren was making friends with a neighborhood cat, and we were just talking."

"The cat ran off a few minutes ago," I explained.

"Oh. Well, do you want to come eat?" Blake asked.

Sean stood and headed for the door. I hoped my dad wouldn't be too hurt if I left, but there was no way I could eat with Leo there, especially knowing how easily I could give us away. "I… um… I need to go. Can you tell my dad something came up? A project for school."

"Sure," Sean said.

"Thanks."

I'd reached the bottom of the porch steps when Sean called out, "Wait. Give me your number."

I told him, and then he sent me a text. "Call me. I'm a decent listener."

"Okay."

Instead of going straight home, I called one of my college friends and ended up playing video games with him all afternoon. Blowing up things on the screen was a great way to keep my mind off Leo. When I was about halfway back to Charlotte, my phone rang. I glanced quickly at the screen and saw Leo's name there. I thought about not answering, but after the reaction I'd had at my dad's house, I knew we needed to talk.

"Leo?"

"Yes, it's me."

"Just checking, since I didn't even know you still had my number." Fuck, I sounded so bitter.

"I guess I deserved that."

"So why are you calling now?"

"Because this is going to keep happening every time we see each other, isn't it?" he asked.

"What exactly do you mean by 'this'?"

"I mean that I'm going to want to strip you down,

bend you over the closest surface, and take you just like I did before."

Holy fucking fuck. I nearly swerved off the road. "Then yes, that's going to keep happening, and I'm going to keep wanting you to do it and falling over tables thinking about it."

He sighed. "That's what I thought."

"Sean knows."

Leo sputtered. "What? How? You didn't—"

"No, I didn't tell him. He saw my reaction to you, and when I explained that I was in a shitty mood because there was a man I wanted and couldn't have, he figured it out."

"He won't tell Graham and Avery, will he?"

"No, assuming they don't guess. He might tell Blake, though."

"Shit. This really isn't going to get any better."

"If they're going to find out anyway, no matter what we do now, shouldn't we just enjoy ourselves?"

He growled. "You're making this even harder to resist."

I hoped that wasn't the only thing that was hard. "I don't want to make it easy. You're the one that refused to consider seeing each other."

"You know damn well why I did."

"Yes, I do. I know my dad has been there for you when you needed him. And I know that if it hadn't been for you when Mom kicked him out… Well, I don't know what would've happened. You made him start enjoying life again. And I'm grateful for that. I was a shit to him. I believed stuff Mom told me instead of talking to him myself. I'm so glad things are better between us now, and I know that being with you puts that at risk, but I also know that you're the man I want, the Dom I want to teach me about everything I'm craving."

I stopped there, heart pounding so hard, I thought I

might have to pull over. I doubted I would've had the courage to say all that to Leo in person, but it felt good to have it out there, even if he—

"I want to be the one to help you discover what you like, what your limits are."

"Y-you do?"

"Yes. I don't have a solution for how to handle things with Graham, but I'm tired of fighting this, and it's not like we won't keep seeing each other like we did today."

"I'm on my way back to Charlotte," I said.

"Back? What do you mean?"

"I started school at UNC Charlotte."

"You did?"

"Yes, I did. At the time I thought it would be great to be close to a certain man I was involved with."

"We had a three-month agreement. You shouldn't—"

"The program is awesome. It's just what I'd hoped it would be when I applied."

"Oh, well… when will you get here?"

"Here as in Charlotte?"

"Yes."

Holy fuck, this was really happening. "I was going to stop and get some dinner on the way, so I'll be at my apartment in about an hour."

"I want you to come to my house instead."

"And how do I know you won't decide things are off again afterwards?" As much as I wanted this, I had to know he wasn't going to push me away again.

"Because I have missed you every minute since you left my place in Asheville. Because there's something between us, something intense, and I need to explore it more. Because I haven't felt this excited about doing a scene with a man in years."

"Oh, wow."

"I'm texting you my address now. When you get here, I want you to strip immediately, and from that moment on, you're mine until I say the scene ends or you use your safeword."

I did pull off the road then. I was going to need a moment to compose myself and program my GPS. "I... um... yes, Sir."

"Good. I'll see you soon."

He ended the call, and I took several deep breaths, hoping to hell I wouldn't regret this.

10

LEO

The knock at my door made me jump. I wasn't expecting Wren for another half hour. I ran to answer it anyway, hoping he was early. I forced myself to take a deep breath before looking through the peephole. Wren was standing there looking very nervous, so I quickly opened the door and gestured for him to step inside.

"You got here fast."

"I was too excited to eat, so I just drove straight through." I loved the way his cheeks had gone pink.

"I'm excited too," I admitted.

"I know it hasn't been that long, but it feels like forever since I was with you."

"Yeah, it does."

We both laughed nervously. Then he began unbuttoning his shirt, and I remembered the instructions I'd given him.

I watched in silence as he stripped with careful movements. I didn't think he was deliberately making a show, but he was taking his time, so I got a slow reveal of all the things I'd been dying to see again. By the time he was naked, I was ready to turn him around, push him against the door, and fuck him until he screamed.

But I'd promised myself something much more drawn out, and I'd regret it if I messed that up. He probably would too. Since I hadn't yet gotten out the toys I intended to use on him, I had to improvise. "While I get everything ready, I want you to kneel right there." I pointed to the rug in front of the couch, and Wren's eyes widened.

"Do you have a problem with that, boy?"

"No, but I have a question first. When you spanked me before, you made a no sex rule. Are you sticking to that today?"

I growled. He was really going to be the death of me. "No, I'm not. Today I'm going to fuck you so hard you'll have trouble walking tomorrow."

He swallowed hard. "That sounds amazing, Sir."

"Yes, it does. Now kneel like you were asked."

He walked slowly across the room and knelt in one fluid motion. I stared at him for several seconds before I could make myself head to the bedroom. As I looked through my toys, I realized I didn't have to wait to get started after all. I picked up some nipple clamps and went back out to the living room.

I knelt in front of Wren and showed him what I'd brought for him. He watched as I pinched one of his nipples and then hissed when I set the first clamp, and I leaned in so I could whisper against his ear. "Are you okay, boy?"

"Yes, Sir."

"Hurts, doesn't it?" I'd chosen some rather vicious clamps, but I knew he could handle them.

"Yes, but I'm f-fine."

I readied his other nipple, and this time he cried out a bit when the clamp pinched him.

I smiled, wanting to reassure him. "You look beautiful like this, boy."

"Thank you, Sir."

"I'm going to go get everything else ready now. I expect you to wait here."

I flicked my fingers against the clamps, making them sway. Wren bit his lip, obviously trying to keep from making a sound.

I cupped his chin and forced him to meet my gaze. "I don't want you to hold anything back. I want every sound. Do you understand?"

"Yes, Sir." He was shaky, and I guessed he was trying to process all that he was feeling, emotionally and physically.

"Use red to stop or yellow to slow down anytime. There's absolutely no shame in needing a break or not enjoying something I do. I only want you to suffer in ways that make you feel good. Okay, boy?"

"Yes, Sir. And this… this does make me feel good. I haven't felt this… grounded in a very long time."

His words made my chest tighten, because I hadn't either. I'd known our connection was special. I couldn't believe I'd almost thrown away the chance to let it grow.

I returned to the bedroom and quickly arranged the things I needed, laying them out so I'd have easy access to them. When I returned to Wren, he was gazing down at the carpet. He looked amazing with his nipples clamped, and the thought of how it would hurt when I removed them and sensation rushed back sent a thrill through me. He was going to love that almost as much as I would love watching.

I held out my hand to him. "I'm ready for you, boy."

He stood, and I led him to the bedroom. "Stretch out on your back, arms up, legs wide. I'm going to restrain your wrists and ankles. Is that okay, boy?"

"Yes. I trust you, Sir."

"I know you do, and I won't let you down."

He arranged himself, and I cuffed his wrists and attached the cuffs to ring bolts in the bed frame. He looked apprehensive, so I caressed his side, trying to soothe him.

"Leo?"

"Yes, baby?"

"Don't leave me."

His words cut through me. "I won't. I swear to you I won't leave you again."

I hoped he knew that I meant more than physically leaving the bedroom. I was in this now, for better or for worse. We were eventually going to have to tell Graham, so he wouldn't find out on his own. I needed to decide how that should happen and how I could salvage our friendship, but tonight, I was just going to focus on Wren.

WREN

WHEN LEO CUFFED my ankles and restrained them, stretching me into a spread-eagle pose, I thought it would make me more nervous. Instead, it settled me. Somehow, knowing I was laid out for him to play with allowed me to just relax.

He gave me a slow once-over.

"Like what you see, Sir?"

He cracked his hand across my thigh. "You won't be smirking like that in a few minutes, boy."

"Oh, really?" My bratty side felt like coming out to play.

"Yes, really."

Leo reached for something he'd placed on a bench at

the end of his bed. It looked a bit like a flashlight with a long glass tube attached to it. "What is that?"

He pressed a button on it. The glass part lit up, and it started to buzz.

"This is a violet wand. It will deliver a light shock when it comes close to your skin. The shock will be intensified by metal, like those clamps."

"Oh, fuck." I stared at the device in his hand, wanting and not wanting to see how it felt.

"I'll start with less sensitive areas."

I nodded. "Yes, Sir."

He skimmed the wand along my legs. The scary snap made me jump, but the shock was lighter than I'd expected. It didn't hurt very much at all. It just made me more aware of whatever part of me was being stimulated. Still, I tensed as he moved closer to my cock. What would it feel like there?

"Leo?" My voice shook.

"Trust me, boy."

I was trying to. He skimmed the wand along my hipbone and up my side. Then he moved closer to my nipples. If it touched the clamps…

"Yellow."

He pulled the wand back and turned it off. "What's wrong?"

"Would you blindfold me, please? I want this. I want to feel it, but the anticipation… it's just too much."

"The anticipation can be part of the fun, but this is your first time, and I want you comfortable."

I nodded. "Thank you, Sir."

"I'm going to step into the closet. I'll be right back."

He returned seconds later with what looked like a sleeping mask.

"Better?" he asked after slipping it over my head.

"Yes, Sir."

"Good. If you change your mind and want me to remove it, just tell me."

"I will."

The wand began to buzz again and I felt the tingling shock along my shoulder, down my arm, across my stomach, and then—holy shit!—right on my cock. I squirmed and bucked. He skimmed it over my shaft again, and I cried out, fighting the restraints.

"Good?" he asked.

I wanted to deny it, but I couldn't. "Fuck, yes, and you know it."

He laughed as he teased my sides and then my thighs. I braced for him to touch my cock again, but instead he slid it over one of the nipple clamps.

I made a strangled sound, the pain taking my breath. I writhed as he touched my abdomen again and then the other nipple.

"Fuck, that hurts!"

He just grinned. "You're so beautiful when you suffer for me."

"More!" It hurt, but my cock was so hard, and I was so… I didn't know how to explain it, but I knew I didn't want him to stop.

He moved the wand more quickly this time, skimming from my cock to my nipple and then running it over my balls. He'd give me short breaks, stimulating my arms or thighs. Then he'd go right back to my nipples. He kept it up until I was sweaty and desperate, begging for something. More? Less? To come? I wasn't even sure.

Leo slid the wand between my legs, teasing my ass.

"Oh, God, are you going to put it inside me?"

"I could. Would you like that?"

"I… I don't think I'm ready for that."

"Okay, baby, we'll save that for another day."

The buzzing stopped. "I think that's enough. I'm going to take the clamps off now."

I'd played with clamps enough to know it was going to hurt when he removed them. He unclamped both sides at the same time, and I arched off the bed, groaning.

"Yes, boy, let me know how it feels."

"It hurts. It fucking hurts."

"And you love it."

"I do. Thank you for knowing that."

He leaned down and kissed me gently. "You're welcome. I'm very proud of you, boy."

"Can you take the blindfold off now?"

He pulled it off and kissed me again, harder this time. I opened my mouth, welcoming him as his tongue thrust into me. A few moments later, he pulled back and looked me up and down. "You're so beautiful, boy. Are you okay?"

"I…" Was I? "I don't know. I… I just need." My cock ached, and I couldn't stop shifting on the bed. All the intensity, all the pain, seemed to have channeled itself into lust now.

Leo pushed my hair back from my face. "I love how much this turns you on."

"Please," I begged, unable to say more.

"I'll help you, baby." He climbed onto the bed, knelt between my spread legs, and took my cock in his hand. When he leaned over and took it in his mouth, I gasped. That was the last thing I expected, but I wasn't about to protest.

He took me to the back of his throat, and I knew I wouldn't last long. Seeing his lips stretched around my cock was almost enough to send me over. He pulled back and teased me, licking and nibbling until I was writhing like I had as he'd sent electricity through me.

"Please," I begged. "Give me more."

He took me all the way to the root, and I gasped. "Fuck, I… I can't hold back."

He pulled off. "I don't want you to. Come in my mouth. Give me every drop."

Holy shit! I only lasted a few seconds more once he started sucking me again. I bucked up, pushing even deeper into his mouth as I shot my load down his throat. He swallowed it all, and that was the hottest fucking thing I'd ever seen. Somehow, despite choking on my cock, Leo looked no less powerful than when he'd been tormenting me.

Once I was thoroughly spent, he let my cock slide from his mouth and licked me clean before sitting back on his heels.

"Was that good, boy?"

I laughed. "Good doesn't even begin to describe it."

LEO

Wren looked amazing all blissed out and relaxed. Sucking him had been even better than I'd expected, and my cock was begging for relief.

"I want to come all over you."

His spent cock stirred as he nodded frantically. "Please."

I unfastened my pants, then grabbed the lube and squirted a bit in my hand as I rose up on my knees. I couldn't take my eyes off him as I worked my cock, faster and faster. This wasn't going to take any time at all, not after tasting him.

"Give it to me, please."

Fuck. Hearing him beg for my cum like that was too much. My breath caught as my balls drew up. Then my hot cum splashed across his body, landing on his cock, his abs, his chest. I pumped myself until I was completely drained.

Wren was looking down at his torso. "It's liked you've marked me, and I'm yours now."

"You are mine, boy."

He looked up, his gaze catching mine. "Am I?"

I nodded, afraid my voice would break if I spoke. I slid my fingers through the mess I'd made and then brought them to my mouth. I sucked the cum from them and then bent down and kissed Wren, feeding it to him.

He groaned against my mouth, trying to deepen the kiss.

"More," he demanded when I pulled back. I gave him exactly what he wanted.

I scooped up more cum, but this time, I held my fingers to his lips. The feel of his hot mouth sucking me clean would've had me hard again if I hadn't just come.

"I want to suck you," he said.

I smiled down at him. "Another time, boy. I don't have your recovery time." I glanced pointedly at his cock, which was fully hard again.

"Then untie me and come hold me while we wait."

I stiffened. I'd held shaky subs after a scene when they needed it, but I'd never been a cuddler. I freed his wrists and then moved toward the end of the bed.

"Leo?"

I looked up at him.

"You're not going to refuse to hold me, are you?"

Oh, fuck. "Not if that's what you need. I'll get you some water and chocolate, and then I'll—"

"I appreciate your attention to aftercare, but I don't

want you to hold me because I'm shaky from the intensity of what we did. I just enjoy being with you."

"Wren, I…" Shit. I was fucking this up, as a Dom, as a lover. But I'd never expected to feel like this, terrified and needy. I'd thought if I ever found someone I wanted for more than some hot scenes, I'd feel confident, not scared to death. Not that I'd ever have imagined I'd fall for my best friend's son. Fall for? Fuck. Was I in love with him?

"You just said I was yours. Did you mean that?"

"I did." But I couldn't admit that I was afraid of feeling too much too soon.

"I know snuggling in bed wasn't part of the original agreement, but that agreement went to hell when I admitted who I was. This is us acting on something we can't fight. Or I can't, anyway, and I thought—"

"Why the hell do you always have to be right?" Of course I couldn't follow the same rules I'd use with anyone else. What I felt for Wren wasn't like anything I'd felt before.

He laughed. "Maybe it's because you need humbling."

"Shit, I probably do."

"So I would like some water and chocolate and the ankle cuffs are starting to chafe, but what I really want most is you."

I quickly undid the cuffs and inspected his ankles to make sure the skin wasn't broken. Then I left just long enough to grab some water and a few Reese's cups and hurried back to the bedroom.

Wren was still lying on his back, but he turned to his side to make it easier to drink the water. I fed him bites of Reese's, which made him smile. When he was done, I pulled a blanket over us and spooned him. He snuggled back against me.

"See? Doesn't this feel good?"

I really did hate how he was always right. "Yes."

"Damn right it does."

I pulled him even tighter against me. "Do you want to stay the night?"

He turned to face me. "Really? You'd let me?"

I nodded. "I'd like it, actually." Now that I was holding him, I didn't want to let him go.

"I'd like it too."

So we fell asleep, spent and sticky, holding on to each other.

11

WREN

I stared at the text I'd just sent Sean, wondering if I'd done the wrong thing by telling him where I'd been the night before.

Three pulsating dots appeared on the screen. I tensed, unable to look away as I waited for his message to pop up: *Go you! How did that happen?*

At least he seemed to approve. *Leo called me a few hours after I left the party.*

My phone rang seconds later. It was Sean.

"I'm too excited to keep typing, so I had to just call you. Go on. Tell me everything." I could easily imagine Sean pacing around his apartment like a hyper Chihuahua.

"Uh-uh. Not everything."

"That good, huh?" I could hear the smile in his voice.

"Better."

Sean made a swoony sigh. "I feel dizzy."

"As if you don't have a hot man to satisfy you."

"I do, annnnd…"

"What?"

"I'm moving in with him," he squealed.

"Sean, that's awesome. So you asked him last night?"

"Yep. Not long after you left. Enough about that, though. Tell me some dirty details."

I laughed. Sean was really something else. "You really think it's okay? Me and Leo being together?"

"I do. I know things will be rocky when you tell Graham."

I pushed a few textbooks out of the way so I could flop down on my bed. "I have no idea how to make him understand."

Sean hummed. "I think you'll have to trust that while he might be mad at first, he'll eventually realize both of you are happy, and that's what he wants for you. Leo does make you happy, right?"

I sighed. "Yes. So much. At first I was worried he'd insist that this was just about sex or, well, sex and dominance."

"Oooh. I do like where this is going."

"Hush." I rolled my eyes even though he couldn't see me. "After he... after we..."

"Yes, do go on."

"After he tied me up and taught me that I like pain as much as I thought I did, I basically forced him to cuddle with me, and he asked me to stay the night."

"You know I would like more details, but wow, that sounds perfect."

I gave a dreamy sigh that made Sean giggle.

"So you're going to see him again?"

"Yes, before I agreed to see him, I told him I couldn't take him walking away again. He said he was done with that."

"Oh, Wren, I'm so happy for you."

"I'm happy too, but it would be better if we didn't have to deal with my dad."

"Do it soon, and get it over with."

Thinking about talking to Dad made me jittery, so I slid off my bed and headed toward the kitchen.

"I'm not sure I'm ready to talk to him, and I know Leo isn't. He's so afraid of losing my dad's friendship. They've been really close for a long time."

"I get that, I do, but he should hear it from you, not someone else. Be sure you don't go to either of Leo's clubs before you tell him. You know your dad and Avery are VIP members, right?"

I grimaced as I grabbed a soda from the fridge. "Avery told me, but please don't make me think about that."

"All right, but just check with Avery so you don't see anything you shouldn't. Whatever you're imagining them doing is probably too tame."

"Wait. Are you saying they play publicly? Where I could see them?"

"Yeah, sorry. At least you know they're accepting of kink, but it also kind of sucks to have family in the scene. I'm glad my mom's not into BDSM, or at least if she is, I'll never have to know about it."

I set the soda down on the coffee table and went to get my laptop and the books I needed to get started on my homework. "I really don't want to talk about this anymore. It's bad enough that Dad knows what Leo likes, and he's going to make assumptions about what we do."

"I wish I could say you're wrong."

"I'll talk to Leo, okay?"

"Okay, and I swear I won't say anything. I haven't even hinted to anyone but Blake, and he already suspected based on things Leo had said to him."

"That's okay. I thought you might tell him, and I'm sorry I'm putting you in this position."

"It's fine. You need someone to talk to who understands."

He was right. I really did.

"Blake expects me to be ready for him in a few minutes, so I've got to run, but call or text me later if you need to talk more or if you want to give me more dirty details."

"No dirty details."

"Dammit. You're no fun."

"Go make Blake happy, and I'll talk to you later. I'll be in Asheville next weekend for our monthly family dinner. Maybe we can hang out then."

"You got it."

I ended the call and sank onto the couch. Talking to Sean really had made me feel better, but it also made me wonder how long Leo and I could keep our relationship a secret. If Blake had guessed, how long before someone else did too?

12

LEO

I spent the late morning hours going over Succumb's monthly expenditures with my bookkeeper—and good friend—Max, but I hadn't heard much of what he was saying. I was too lost in memories of the night before—Wren and I had focused on anal play, and I'd gotten him to take a huge ribbed anal cone. It had been so intense that Wren wasn't the only one who cried at the end of the scene.

I couldn't believe Wren and I had been seeing each other for a month now. We'd typically only gotten together once a week because of his heavy load at school, but that had been enough time to learn a lot about each other. I was more sure than ever that we were perfect for each other, but we still had to keep our relationship a secret. We were both feeling the weight of that deception.

I knew Max had noticed how inattentive I was, and I was also certain he'd listen if I could force myself to open up. But I'd never been good at talking about anything too personal. One of my father's first lessons was that men never showed emotions. My father didn't think "real" men fucked other men either, which was how I'd ended up not speaking to him for the last twenty years.

Somehow, despite that early programming, I'd been able to open up to Graham. He was always the one I went to when something was bothering me. He was probably the only person other than Wren who'd ever heard me admit that I was scared. And now that I was facing the scariest thing in my life—falling for someone I wasn't meant to have—I couldn't talk to Graham.

Was I making this connection with Wren far more dramatic than it was? No, what I was feeling was real. If Graham and Blake could know they were in love in a matter of days, then it could happen to me too. Wren was The One for me. I was certain of it.

"Leo, are you listening?" Max asked.

"What? Oh, sorry. I…"

He closed his laptop and narrowed his eyes at me. "You've been distracted and edgy for weeks. When are you going to tell me what's up?"

I started to brush off his concern. Max was as close or closer to Graham than he was to me. Was it fair to ask him to keep my secret?

"Leo, come on, talk to me."

"If I do, I'll have to ask you to keep what I say secret, especially from Graham."

Max frowned. He knew how close Graham and I were.

"I shouldn't ask you—"

"No, it's okay, and it's obvious you need to share this with someone."

"I have a new sub."

"Okay, and this is a problem why?" Max was obviously puzzled.

"My sub is Graham's son, Wren."

He blinked, started to say something, then closed his mouth and just stared.

"Yeah. So that's why it's a problem."

"Oh, wow."

"You're not helping."

He winced. "Sorry. I'm just a bit shocked."

"This isn't just a casual thing, and it's not something either of us planned. God, that sounds so fucking lame."

"Graham and Wren weren't talking to each other for a long time, right?"

"Right, which just makes the situation worse."

Max nodded. "So when you say it's not casual, you've never really been casual about taking on subs, so—"

"I think I'm in love with him."

Max sucked in his breath. "Well, fuck."

"Exactly."

"I know you probably don't want to hear this, but if this is serious, not a short-term thing, you've got to tell Graham."

I knew he was right. Wren thought we needed to go ahead and tell him too, but I hadn't felt ready yet. "He's going to fucking hate me."

Max frowned. "Do you really think that? How long have you two been friends?"

"Eight years."

"And from what he's told me, you basically put him back together after his divorce."

I frowned, not wanting to be made out to be anyone's savior. "Maybe, more or less, but—"

"You were his anchor."

"And now I'm fucking his son." Max opened his mouth to respond, but I kept going. "It's not even just that. Graham knows what I like, what I want from my subs. He's going to think I'm hurting his son, and he's going to be right."

Max's brows went down. "How old is Wren?"

"Twenty-two."

"And I'm sure you've had his explicit consent for everything you've done."

"Well, yeah, but—"

"And whose idea was it for you to play together the first time?" Max asked.

"His, but Graham isn't going to care about that."

Max seemed to consider that. "Maybe not at first. He might need a while to process everything, but he knows how much you value consent. He isn't going to think you've coerced Wren into something he didn't seek out himself."

"Are you sure this is okay? Is it wrong of me to even consider being with Wren? I keep wondering if I'm just a selfish bastard."

Max laid a hand on my shoulder. "One thing I learned after almost missing out on a relationship with Elliot is that when you want something—when you know it's the right thing for you—you have to be willing to ask for it. If Elliot hadn't come after me, I'd still be avoiding his food truck and wishing I could meet someone who would love me just the way I am."

I didn't think I'd ever heard Max say that much at once. He was usually the quiet, observant one when we got together with friends, though as usual his words were thoughtful and wise.

"So you're saying I need to show Wren I'm serious, and we need to tell Graham ASAP."

Max gave me a soft smile. "I am, but I don't mean to act like I think that will be easy."

"Graham is going to be furious."

"Possibly, but he'll get over it. He cares too much about you to do otherwise."

Did he? "I hope so."

Max studied me. "There's something else bothering you."

"Should I have gone easy on Wren since he's young, and he's Graham's, and—"

"You mean, should you have refused to give him what he asked for?"

I nodded, though phrased that way it sounded wrong.

"Would the two of you have an honest relationship if you did that?"

"No."

"Exactly. If I did a scene with a Dom who insisted I didn't know what I wanted—I don't mean just starting slowly but someone who babied me—I wouldn't see him again. If you hold back, you won't make Wren happy."

Max was abso-fucking-lutely right. "Thank you."

"You're welcome. Whenever you tell Graham, no matter how he reacts at first, remember that when he's thinking clearly, he wants the best for both of you."

"I don't think he's ever going to believe I'm the right man for his son."

"Don't be so sure." Max pushed his chair back and stood. "Come on."

"Where are we going?"

"Elliot's got his truck at Charlotte Brews tonight. We're going to go get some spicy food and beer."

I had too much work to get done to take a long lunch. "I don't—"

"When was the last time you just let yourself relax and stop worrying about Thrust, Succumb, and all the other burdens you take on yourself?"

I frowned. Never? "Um… I don't know."

"And now you've added a stressful relationship to everything you have to worry about. It's no wonder you've been on edge. You're going to drive yourself crazy if you keep this up, and you won't be any good to Wren."

"Fine." I stood to join him. He wasn't going to let this go. Max might be fairly reserved, but he was also persistent. "Elliot really must be treating you right, because you're way more relaxed than I've ever seen you."

He gave me a goofy grin. "He is everything I could have wished for."

"I'm so happy for you."

"Things could be like this for you and Wren."

"Or Graham could never speak to me again, and Wren could decide being with me is too divisive. And it's not like we can go out with Graham and Avery. How weird would that be?"

Max shook his head. "You doing a scene in front of them would be weird; going out for beers would not."

"Oh my God. I cannot even think about them seeing us at Succumb or…" I shuddered, trying to push those thoughts away.

Max laughed. "That would be bad, but dinner together would work. Graham and Avery do that with Carter and Felicity."

"Yes, but Felicity doesn't want to do cruel things to Carter just to watch him squirm and beg, and she's not been friends with Graham for—"

"Don't you think it's weird for Carter having his dad living with Felicity's best friend, a man his own age, who if my guess is right will soon technically be his stepdad?"

"You think Graham is going to propose?" I'd been wondering when that would happen.

He grinned. "It wouldn't surprise me."

"No, me either. He's so in love with Avery, but it's still different and—"

Max held up his hand. "We've analyzed enough. It's time to focus on beer, food, and relaxation."

"Seriously, where did all this zen come from?"

"Elliot is really good at easing my tension when he's not overworking himself on the truck."

We both laughed and then I drew Max into a hug. "Thank you for listening."

"Any time."

We spent the rest of the evening talking about my plans for Thrust and an upcoming demo night at Succumb, at least when Max wasn't too busy staring at his man as he worked up a sweat in his food truck.

13

LEO

My doorbell rang on Friday night, and I rushed to answer it, hoping it was Wren arriving early because he was as eager for this night as I was. It had been almost a week since we'd seen each other. Both our schedules were usually too crazy for any weeknight dates.

When I opened the door and saw him standing there, looking amazing, I grabbed his hand and pulled him inside.

"Need you," he groaned as he gripped my hips, pulling me tightly against himself.

A quickie in the entryway wasn't part of my plan for the night, but I decided I didn't care. I unzipped his jeans, then mine, and wrapped my hand around both our cocks.

He hissed. "Jesus, Leo, I—"

"Just feel," I told him. "Don't worry about anything else."

I always planned my encounters with men instead of just letting need take over. But now I was giving in to lust with Wren just like I had the first time I'd fucked him. I so rarely got off without any games or role play, but with

Wren, the only thing that mattered was that we were both happy.

I kept working our dicks as I kissed Wren's jaw, his neck, his ear. He begged, "More, please. I just... I..."

"I know what you need."

"You always do. That's why I couldn't walk away."

I gripped our shafts tightly, working them with sure strokes until Wren bucked into my fist, crying out as he came. Even then I didn't stop.

"Too much," he whined.

"But I'm not done touching you."

"Oh, fuck." He laid his head on my shoulder, panting as I smeared his cum along our shafts, using it to ease my way. He whimpered, but he didn't protest again.

I was so ready to come, but I held myself back, trying to draw this out. Wren had never gone fully soft, and now he was hardening again, even though he was still making small sounds of protest.

"I want to watch you come." His voice was rough with need. "I want..."

"What do you want, baby?"

"I want to taste you."

Suddenly I wanted that more than I could say. I let go of our cocks. "Kneel."

Wren dropped to his knees immediately.

"Hands behind your back."

He looked up, his expression unsure, but he obeyed anyway.

"I don't want to hold back. I want to use your mouth, to choke you with my dick. I—"

"Please. I want that too."

I took hold of my cock and brushed his lips with it, wishing I wasn't so close to the edge already. I considered going to get a cock ring, but I didn't want to risk breaking the mood between us. Toying with his soft curls, I asked, "Have you done this before?"

"Sucked cock? Yeah, I—"

"No, been thoroughly face fucked."

His cheeks pinkened. "No, but I want to."

I was thrilled that I'd be the first man to do this to him. "If you need me to stop, just tap my thigh."

"Yes, Sir."

He groaned around me as I pushed into his mouth, and I had to clamp down on the urge to come as I kept going, feeding him my cock. I could tell he was struggling to take it all. I wanted to drive in all the way, watch him choke, make him fight to breathe, but he wasn't ready for that. When he swallowed around me, I nearly came.

"Fuck, you look so hot, boy. I love having you on your knees."

He sucked me and rubbed my underside with his tongue.

I gave him more, and he gagged. I pulled partway out, but he still didn't tell me to stop, so I pushed back in, not stopping this time until his nose brushed my abdomen.

"You're so fucking beautiful with your mouth stuffed so full."

He sputtered around me, and I knew he was struggling to breathe. I held him there another second and then pulled back.

He gasped for air, and I gave him just enough time to catch his breath before driving back in, harder this time. I could tell he wanted to fight it, but he kept his hands behind his back and let me have control. His surrender awed me. I tried to make myself go easy on him, but as Wren figured out how to relax and take my full length more easily, I couldn't hold back. I thrust into him over and over. Then, with a shout, I came down his throat. He swallowed around me, clearly trying to get every drop. When I pulled out, he smiled dreamily, and I dropped to my knees and pulled him into my arms.

"I think…" His voice was hoarse from my rough use. "I think this thing between us is a lot more than just exploring kink."

Did he think I thought that was all it was? "You're right, baby. It's so much more." Part of me still worried that being with him was wrong, but I'd fallen for him, and there wasn't any way to change that. "I want it to be more."

The smile he gave me melted my heart. "So this is real? All this that I'm feeling?"

"It's the realest thing I've ever known."

"We have to tell him." We both said the words at the same time.

I laughed, unable to help myself, and Wren joined me until we were shaking so hard we had to lean on each other to stay upright.

"Shit. This shouldn't be so funny," Wren said.

"I know, but…"

"You're really close to my dad, aren't you?" Wren asked. "I don't think I quite understood how much the two of you mean to each other."

I nodded. "I don't talk to any of my family, and Graham's been the most important person in my life for a while now."

Wren paled, and I regretted saying that. "Have you…? Shit. Were you and my dad…?"

"Not in years. And never for anything but comfort. We don't… fit as lovers."

"Yeah, I didn't think he was much of a submissive."

I laughed. "No, he's not. Are you okay with this? I know it makes our whole situation even weirder for you."

Wren considered his answer for a moment, but finally he smiled. "It's okay. I'm not sure our family situation could get much more fucked up."

"Fucked up or not, you're lucky to have family who cares."

"Yeah. I know. So how are we going to do this, tell my dad I mean? And when?"

I wanted to put it off, but I knew we couldn't. "Graham is coming to Charlotte next weekend; maybe then." Part of me wanted Wren to say it was too soon.

"All right. I guess that's good. I could tell him tomorrow, but I think we should do it together."

"Yes, we should."

Wren let out a shaky breath. "Do we have to figure out what to say now?"

"No. Tonight should be about us. We're going to eat the takeout I ordered, and then I'm going to work you over with my favorite flogger."

His eyes widened. "Yes, please. I need that."

"So do I."

WREN

AFTER WE FINISHED the Thai takeout Leo had gotten us, we needed to let our food settle, so we curled up on the couch and turned on a movie. I laid my head on Leo's shoulder, and he wrapped his arms around me, holding me close. I hardly paid any attention to the TV, content to close my eyes and revel in how warm and loved I felt. I'd started this whole thing with Leo because I wanted to explore new things. I'd never expected to learn that I needed to be held and cared for as much as I needed pain. Leo turned and looked down at me.

"Is this okay? I know I told you I'd—" I placed a finger on his lips.

"Let's just stay like this for now."

Leo nodded and took my hand in his. I tried to watch the movie, but I ended up dozing, more relaxed than I'd been in a long time.

When the credits started to roll, Leo pressed pause, and I forced myself to sit up as I said, "I hope you didn't mind that we weren't—"

"I didn't mind at all. I hadn't realized how much I needed this, just being with someone I can sit with in silence without it feeling awkward. I'm sorry I tried to push you away."

"You were scared. I was scared too. I still am, but…"

"We'll figure this out together." Hearing him say that made me even warmer than cuddling with him had.

"Was this enough for you tonight, or do you still want to—"

I rose up on my knees and took his face in my hands. "I want you to show me everything."

"Everything?" He raised his brows. "I don't think we have time for that tonight."

I grinned at him. "Then we'll need more time."

"Which is just fine, because I have no intention of letting you go."

"Kiss me," I demanded, and he did.

It took us a while to move from the couch to the bedroom. I wanted something harsher from him than these sweet kisses, but holding him against me felt so good, I wasn't about to protest.

When Leo finally coaxed me to the bedroom, he maneuvered me until I was standing by the bed.

"I want you to stay completely still and only move when I tell you to. Can you do that for me?"

Leo held my gaze, and my heart pounded as I chewed my lower lip. I'd told him I just wanted to be tormented, not controlled, but now the thought of obeying him had me so fucking hot, partly because I knew he wanted my submission, and I wanted to please him. "Yes, I can do that, Sir."

"Good boy."

I could be good for him. I hadn't been sure I was good for anyone before he'd touched me the first time, but seeing him so content with me, so ready to give me more, had affected me, even more than the rush of endorphins from the pain he'd given me.

Leo took hold of my shirt and began pushing it up my chest very slowly. I started to raise my arms so he could pull it over my head, but he slapped my thigh. "I didn't tell you to move."

"I just—"

Another slap. This one harder.

"Yes, Sir."

He bent and licked my nipple. I shivered, anticipating a bite, but he simply shifted to the other side, licking the other tightened bud then blowing against it. His cool breath made my nipples harden more. He sucked at them in turn, tugging, pulling, giving me just a hint of teeth, before pulling away. "Sometimes anticipation is almost as good as the pain."

Shit. I'd forgotten he was a master at this.

"Lift your arms." He pulled my shirt off and tossed it onto a chair. "Arms down now."

I lowered them and held my breath as he let his gaze slowly roam over my chest and abdomen. I was quickly learning how right he was. Anticipation could be just as unnerving as anything else he might do to me. By the time he reached for my belt, my cock was begging to be freed from the confines of my pants. Slowly—oh so slowly—he lowered my zipper. When he slipped his hands into my waistband and pushed my jeans and briefs down, my cock sprang free, the tip glistening with precum.

"Mmm. You're so eager." Leo smiled and then looked up at me. "You want to know a secret?"

I swallowed before answering. "Um… yes."

He dropped to his knees in front of me. "So am I."

I sucked in my breath, desperate for him to put his mouth on me, but he wrapped his hand around the back of my knee and tugged gently. "Lift your leg."

I did, and he slid my jeans and briefs off and then removed my sock before repeating his request on the other side. Finally, I stood before him completely naked.

He leaned forward, and I tensed. Was he going to suck me now? He ran his tongue along my inner thigh, almost to where my pelvis joined my leg. Then he nibbled tiny bits of skin, rolling them between his teeth. The pleasure/pain went right to my cock, making it jump.

He grinned up at me. "You're perfect."

Heat rushed to my face. "I—"

He shook his head. "No talking. I want you to lie over the end of the bed, but stay far enough back that your cock can't touch the mattress."

My legs shook as I made my way to the bed. I was thankful I would get to have the mattress supporting me, because I didn't think I'd be able to stand while Leo flogged me. I was far too excited, too needy, and a little bit scared. What if it was more than I could take? What if I ended up not liking it? Leo must've sensed how uneasy I was. He laid his hands on my shoulders and pressed his fingers into my tense muscles, massaging me.

"It's okay," he said, his voice low and soft. "I don't have any expectations. Just relax and let me work you over. If you don't like it, use your safeword, and we'll do something else, or nothing at all. This is all about trying things out."

"But this is what you like, and if I don't—"

"No, what I like is you. We're good for each other, and we'll find a way to make things work, no matter what your preferences are."

"How did I get so lucky?"

"Because you're lucky enough to have an amazing father who chose an amazing boyfriend who knew exactly what you needed."

I scowled at him. "Please don't talk about my dad right now."

He just laughed. "I won't mention him again, but I need you to know that somehow, this is all going to be okay."

"I don't expect you to solve this by yourself. I know you're a Dom and everything, but I also know you don't have all the answers."

"If only all subs knew that."

"I told you I'm not really…" Except maybe I'd been wrong.

"Let's not worry about labels. Right now, all I want is to find out what feels good to you—or so bad that it's good."

"Yes, Sir." I positioned myself on the bed, arms stretched out, chest supported by the mattress, waiting and ready.

14

LEO

I looked down at Wren as he arched his back, offering his ass to me. I loved how impatient he was, how needy. I picked up the flogger I'd chosen. It had soft deerskin falls, but I could still make it sting using the right technique. I swirled it over his ass, letting him feel the strands.

"This flogger isn't made to give much pain. My goal right now is just to warm you up, so relax into the mattress and just feel. Do you think you can stay in position without being restrained?"

"Yes, Sir."

He worked his hips, silently begging me to swat his ass. I dangled the flogger over his back, letting the falls just brush his skin, teasing him. He whimpered, and I rewarded that gorgeous sound by bringing the flogger down on his ass several times in quick succession, snapping it hard on the last stroke. He fisted his hands in the sheet as he writhed and moaned. "More. Please."

I swatted his thighs a few times and then his shoulders. I flicked the falls gently over his back, just stimulating the skin, making him anticipate harder blows. Then I slapped his ass again, alternating soft and hard blows until he was shifting restlessly. "Please, Leo. I… Please."

"What do you want?"

"I…"

Before he could come up with an answer, I gave a quick flick of my wrist, landing a stinging blow on his ass. Then I repeated it on the same spot.

"Fuck. More. More of that."

"You like the sting, don't you?"

"Please, yes."

"Should I switch to a more intense flogger now?"

"Yes, Sir."

I examined the other floggers I'd laid out and chose the best one for stinging blows. It had a combination of suede and oiled leather falls, all thin, and it could be quite intense depending on how it was used. I picked it up and tested it in my hand, swishing it through the air to tease him with the whippy sound.

I was an experienced flogger. I'd taught numerous other Doms how to use these implements, and I'd used them on plenty of subs as well as Doms who needed to learn what it would feel like when they used a flogger themselves. But I'd never felt like I did right then. The stakes seemed so much higher with Wren. I needed to be sure I made this as good as possible.

He turned to look at me. "Is everything okay?"

I let out a breath and smiled at him, because suddenly it was. "Yes. I'm fine." I held up the flogger for him to see. "This one's going to sting a lot more. Are you ready?"

He nodded, so I smacked his ass, making him yelp.

"I told you it would sting."

"Fuck, yes it does."

For a few moments, I worked him over using a technique that reduced the impact. Then without warning, I flicked the flogger in a way that made the blow especially intense.

He cried out. "Fuck, that's good."

"You like it?"

"Yes! Don't go easy on me. I'll use my safeword if I need to."

I gave him what he wanted, flogging his ass and then his thighs and back. I stayed in the safe zones but let him feel the sting of the falls on as much of his body as he could.

Then I returned to his ass, concentrating on his already sore flesh until I could see tears on his cheeks. But as much as it was obviously hurting him, he held his position, never doing more than lifting a foot or tugging on the sheet when the flogger came down. His cock was hard and he'd not given any signs of wanting to stop. Still, I paused and laid my hand on his back.

"Wren, are you okay?"

"Yes, I feel… I don't know… It's so good, and I just…"

He seemed to be so deep in subspace he couldn't form full sentences. "It's okay, baby. You don't have to explain." I ran my hand over his ass, letting my fingers graze his crack. "Do you need more?"

"I don't know. I… I just need you."

I wrapped my fingers around his cock and stroked, using the precum that was dripping from his slit like lube. I loved that he was still hard after I'd worked him over so thoroughly.

When I pressed a finger against his hole, he groaned. "Maybe it's time for something else."

WREN

I WHIMPERED as Leo's finger slid inside me. I could no longer really separate pain from pleasure; all sensation just seemed... more. Earlier my back and ass had burned like they'd been lit on fire, but now everything seemed muted except for the ache in my cock. I was going to come any second if Leo kept this up. Before I could warn him, he pushed his finger deeper and brushed my prostate. "Fuck!"

"I am going to fuck you, and you're going to love it."

"Yes. Please."

He drew his other hand down my back, making me wince as he slid over tender flesh. Then he pressed down on what must have been a serious welt on my ass.

I jerked away. "Fuck, that hurts."

"You're even more beautiful with my marks on you."

"Oh, God. Really?"

"Yes, baby." His voice was low and husky, and it made me shiver.

"I feel so warm now, so..." What was I feeling? "So cared for. Is that wrong?"

"No. It's not wrong at all. I am taking care of you, baby. This is what you need. And it's okay, because I need it too. That makes us good together."

"Fuck me, Leo. Please, I need you."

The sounds I heard next told me he was undoing his pants and then opening a condom. Seconds later he was there, teasing my hole with the tip of his cock. My ass was so sore that it was going to hurt when he pressed inside.

"Are you going to take my cock, boy?"

"Yes, Sir. Want to."

He gripped my hips and drove in, making me gasp. "Don't come until I say you can."

I had no idea if I could actually hold off. Leo drove into me again and again, and I pushed back into him, unable to help myself. He tilted my hips, so he could slide in just right to hit my prostate.

"Fuck! So close, so close I can't…"

"You can hold back, baby. I know you can."

I whined as he pulled out and then pushed back in slowly, remembering how hard it had been to let him hear those vulnerable sounds when he'd first spanked me. This time, I just let go.

I begged and cried for him as he fucked me hard, and I fought the need to come. He pounded into me relentlessly. The friction against my ass, the pressure where he gripped my sore shoulders was too much. I writhed under him, sobbing because I needed to come so badly.

Finally, he reached under me and took my dick in his hand. "Come for me, baby."

Seconds later, I did, shouting his name as I went over the edge. Pain and pleasure mingled, and stars flashed in front of my eyes. Then I collapsed against the mattress and darkness took me.

I wasn't sure how long I'd been lying there when I heard Leo calling my name.

"Wren? Wren! Are you okay?"

I forced myself to open my eyes. "'M fine." I wanted to say more, but my brain and mouth didn't seem to be working together. Leo helped me up onto the bed and I curled on my side.

"I'll be right back. I promise."

"'K."

I closed my eyes, and a moment later, he said, "Here." He was holding up a water bottle. "Take at least a few sips."

I realized he'd put a straw in it, and somehow that small gesture made tears sting my eyes. He cupped my chin and lifted my head so I looked at him. "I'm here to take care of you, whether that's with water or with a flogger or by holding you."

"Thank you."

He leaned down and kissed me gently. "Now turn over on your stomach so I can put some salve on you."

I winced when he touched my back, but the cool salve soothed me. I took slow, careful breaths as Leo worked his way down my body, managing to only flinch a few times.

"I'm so proud of you," he said as he rubbed the salve into the sorest part of my ass. "You took far more than I expected for someone new to this. I really hope I didn't push too far."

I shook my head. "It was so good. I wanted everything you gave me." I turned my head, trying to see the marks on my ass.

"When you're ready to stand up, I'll take you to the bathroom and help you see them, if you want."

"Okay. Do you have chocolate for me first?"

He chuckled. "Of course I do."

"I'm sure I'll be able to stand after I have some."

"Are you?"

I nodded. "Chocolate fixes everything."

He finished with the salve and told me to turn back onto my side. Then he handed me a chocolate almond bar. "How's this?"

"Perfect." When I took the first bite, I realized I was really hungry. I ended up gobbling down the whole bar at an embarrassing speed.

"You really did need that," Leo said.

"Yeah, I guess you took a lot out of me."

"I did. You need to drink a lot more water and get plenty of rest tonight."

"Rest here with you?" I asked.

"Yes, baby."

"Good. I want to be close to you." I eased off the bed, but when my ass slid along the sheets I gasped. "Wow. That really hurts."

"You're going to be sore for a while."

"I'm glad I don't have to sit in class tomorrow."

"I would never have gone this far on a weeknight."

He helped me stand. Walking wasn't at all pleasant, but I was determined to make it to the bathroom. Not only did I want to see my back and ass, my bladder was feeling far too full.

When we reached the en suite bathroom, Leo looked for a hand mirror while I relieved myself. Then he turned me around, putting my back to the vanity, and held up the smaller mirror so I could see myself.

"Holy shit!" There were stripes on my upper back and over my ass. I hadn't realized Leo was making a pattern, but the lines were very precise. I rose up on tiptoe to see my thighs, but contracting my leg muscles hurt like hell.

"It's a good idea for you to walk around a bit so you don't stiffen up," Leo said.

"You're really fucking talented, aren't you?" I kept staring, unable to believe how pretty the marks were.

He frowned. "I thought you knew that already, and that's why you trusted me."

"I knew you'd be safe and respectful, but these lines are… wow."

He smiled, obviously pleased with himself.

I took one more look at myself; my ass was so red, and —"Oh fuck, I have to drive to Asheville on Sunday."

"It will help you remember me on the way."

"I don't think I'm going to be forgetting you for a second." Leo frowned, and I could tell he was worried about something. "What's wrong?"

"You're going to be sore, and you'll be having lunch with Graham, and—"

"If he notices anything, I'll just tell him I did a hard workout this weekend." I laid a hand on Leo's arm. "Really, it's fine."

He nodded. "There's no way he'll know, but I just… It's one thing that I'm going out with you, but if he knew I'd done this to you…"

I hated how sad Leo looked. "I asked for this, and I loved it. My dad will have to accept our relationship for what it is."

"You're right. I'm sorry. I was doing fine about it, and then…"

"This isn't easy for either of us, but I love what you did to me. I love how my body looks with your marks on it. I never really thought I'd find someone who could do this for me, and I can't thank you enough, I—" Leo put his finger on my lips.

"You don't need to thank me. I've loved every minute of my time with you. Now. I'm going to feed you—because I could tell you were hungry when you ate the chocolate bar—and then put you to bed."

"I like the sound of all of that, especially if you'll be coming to bed with me."

He smiled. "How else would I hold you while you fell asleep?"

His words did things to my heart that worried me. I'd fallen hard for him, and I didn't think I'd ever want to let him go.

15

WREN

My dad was out checking some properties he was thinking of buying when I arrived at his and Avery's house. I'd left myself plenty of time before lunch with him and my siblings, because with my ass and back still sore, I wanted to wear something more comfortable for the drive than the appropriate clothes for the fine dining restaurant my brother had chosen. I'd put on my dress pants and was reaching for my shirt when I heard the guest room door creak, followed by a gasp.

I turned to see Avery standing in the doorway, staring at me. At least it wasn't my dad.

"I'm so sorry. The bathroom door was closed, and I thought you were in there. You left a sweater here the last time you stayed over, so I was going to put it with your bag." He glanced at me and then back down at the sweater. "I should never have just come in like that."

"It's okay. I know you didn't mean to, but… um…" I knew what he'd seen, but I wasn't sure what to say. I could just pretend nothing was up, but I didn't want him to worry about me.

Avery gave a sheepish smile. "I guess you found someone to experiment with, and… fuck, I'm usually a lot better at talking about sex, but you're like…"

"Your pseudo-stepson?"

"That's just… no. I totally don't think of you that way."

I nodded. "This whole fucking situation is weird."

Avery frowned, and I worried I'd hurt him.

"I don't mean… You make my dad happy, and I'm glad that you're together."

"Thanks. I'm glad you've been exploring, but I feel like… as a friend… I should make sure you're okay. That looks very intense."

I tried not to get annoyed. I knew he truly cared about me. "It's fine. Leo knows what he's doing."

Avery's eyes went wide, and I realized what I'd blurted out. Oh, fuck. I'd ruined everything. I'd promised Leo I wouldn't say anything while I was up here, and now Avery knew, and he would tell Graham, and… "Please don't say anything. I know that's a lot to ask, but I didn't mean to say that. I…"

"I won't tell Graham. I actually think this is a good thing. Leo will take care of you, and you'll be good for him too."

"Except for the whole he's-my-dad's-best-friend thing."

Avery frowned. "Yeah, that's a bit of an issue."

I still couldn't believe I'd just told him about Leo. My pulse pounded in my ears, and the room began to spin. Avery took my arm and helped me sit down on the bed. "Are you okay? Do you need me to get you some water or something?"

"No, I… I'm fine. Or I will be."

He studied me for a moment. "All right, but you're really pale."

"I really like him. Leo. Not just because he's an incredible Dom. I like everything about him."

"Then you need to tell your dad."

"Leo and I are working on a plan for that."

"Good, because you won't be able to hide this for long. He's going to find out eventually."

"You could slip up like I did." *Please don't let that happen.*

"Hopefully not, but who else knows?"

"Sean and Blake."

Avery's mouth dropped open. "Seriously?"

"Sean guessed it after I had a bit of a meltdown at your housewarming, but he swore he wouldn't tell anyone but Blake."

"So that's why you left the party so early."

Heat filled my cheeks as I nodded. "I was afraid I'd give myself away."

Avery gave me a sympathetic look. "I understand, but please tell him soon."

"We will. I promise."

"With me, Sean, and Blake knowing, someone will eventually slip up." Avery glanced at my back again. "Leo's really skilled. I mean, I knew he was, but wow. And you must be…"

"The pain slut Leo's been looking for?"

Avery burst out laughing. "Wow. Yeah, I guess you are, but don't say that when you tell Graham."

"Oh, God, no. Imagine the look on his face."

We both cracked up, and I was able to truly breathe for the first time since Avery had opened my door.

"Avery? Wren?"

"Oh, shit. Graham's home." Avery jumped up and headed toward the door.

So much for feeling more relaxed. I grabbed my shirt,

stuffed my arms into the sleeves, and had it mostly buttoned when my dad appeared in the doorway.

"Sorry I'm not quite ready," I said. "I didn't want to drive in the clothes I was wearing to lunch, and Avery and I started chatting, and…" Shit, I was rambling and my fingers were all fumbly with my buttons. He was going to wonder what I was so nervous about.

"Are you all right?" Dad asked. "You look kind of pale."

"He's fine."

"I'm fine." My words and Avery's ran together.

Dad narrowed his eyes. "What's going on?"

"Nothing." Avery sounded like he actually meant the opposite.

My dad gave me an even more suspicious look. "Leo sounded strange too when I talked to him earlier."

I made a strangled sound that I tried to cover with a cough. "Sorry. My throat's dry."

Avery gave me a worried glance. I was going to fuck this up if I didn't get myself together fast.

Dad frowned at both of us. "Blake was a little strange too when I ran into him. If it was close to my birthday, I might think someone was planning a surprise party."

"Do you want a surprise party?" Avery was clearly trying to change the subject.

"No, not really."

"I'd plan one for you if you did." The way my dad smiled at Avery left no doubt how sickeningly in love the two of them were. "Of course, now that we've talked about it, it wouldn't really be a surprise."

My dad frowned. "It doesn't matter. My birthday is months away."

"You know," Avery interrupted, "Blake was probably

just in a bad mood, because of Sean. Having to put up with him would make anyone weird."

"That's right," I said. "I wouldn't want to put up with Sean all the time."

Graham narrowed his eyes at us. "Something is definitely up with you two. And I'm going to figure it out."

I really hoped he wouldn't. I pushed my feet into my shoes and finished tucking my shirt in. "It's probably time for us to go."

My dad looked at his watch. "It is. I'm going to run to the bathroom, and I'll meet you downstairs."

Avery collapsed back onto the bed after Dad left. "That was painful. I suck at lying to him."

"I know, and I would never ask you to in any other situation. I'm really sorry I'm putting you in this position, especially after you helped me."

"It's all right," Avery said. "I'm glad I was able to help, and I do think you and Leo are good for each other. Things will work out. You'll see."

I studied him for a moment. "Wait. Did you see this coming?"

His eyes widened. "What do you mean?"

"When you called Leo, did you think we'd end up together?"

Avery shook his head. "No. I mean, that's not why I called him. He really was the best person to help, but it did cross my mind that you two would probably hit it off."

"Avery!"

"Once you tell Graham, I'll work on him. I can help him see how good you two are for each other. Both of you deserve someone who truly cares."

I frowned, not sure even Avery would be able to fix this mess. "Thank you, I guess."

"Wren? Are you coming?" my dad called.

"Yeah. I'll be right down."

Avery hugged me. "Good luck."

"Hopefully I can keep my mouth shut better than I did with you."

16

WREN

The family dinner was torture. Back when my dad first insisted the four of us get together once a month, I'd pretended I was too cool for it. Then I realized I actually enjoyed the chance to catch up with Mandy, Carter, and, eventually, even my dad. But today my ass and back hurt, and I was nervous that I was going to fuck up and give myself away.

The restaurant Carter had chosen had a patio. Everyone else wanted to sit outside, so I ended up on the world's most uncomfortable metal chair. I winced every time I shifted, and my dad kept giving me odd looks. He didn't seem to be buying my story that I'd worked out too hard this week. I wasn't sure what he thought was up. Surely he hadn't guessed.

Somehow I made it through the entire meal without blurting out something about Leo. He only came up in conversation once, and I focused on my steak tacos the entire time. As soon as I could politely leave, I did. My insistence that I had a lot of homework was even true. I should have been working on a project while I was spending the weekend with Leo, but staying up late to finish it was a small price to pay for what he'd given me.

My classes were all getting more intense, and I was determined to do my best, so the week flew by in a whirl-wind of lectures, study groups, and projects. I talked to Leo several times, but when Friday arrived, we still hadn't figured out what to say to my dad, though we both agreed we needed to tell him the next day. Leo had brunch plans with him, and I was going to meet them at the restaurant.

My stomach flip-flopped when I imagined Dad's reac-tion, but Avery, Sean, and Leo's friend Max all agreed we were doing the right thing. My conscience did too. There was no way I could go to another family dinner and pretend there was nothing new in my life besides school.

When I showed up at Leo's, I expected him to have ordered takeout, but no food smells greeted me, and Leo was wearing a button-up, a blazer, and—fuck me—were those suspenders? I'd never seen him that dressed up. He looked good enough to eat.

Before I could ask what was up, he said, "I'd like to take you to dinner."

"But I thought—"

"I know we agreed not to go out in public until we told Graham, but we're telling him tomorrow, so what differ-ence will it make if we see someone we know at dinner? Anyone who'd be inclined to tell Graham right away already knows."

I smiled at him. "You're right. And I'd love to go out." I'd understood his reasoning for not dating publicly, but I realized now how important it was to me that this felt like a true relationship rather than a dirty secret. "So where are we going?"

"Max's boyfriend Elliot has an Asian fusion food truck,

Lotus on Wheels, and the food is truly amazing. He'll be at Contempo Wine tonight."

"Oh, that's close to my apartment. I've seen it when I've been hanging out in Ludlow Park. I like to go there and just sit sometimes."

"We should go to the park together sometime, but tonight I thought I'd introduce you to Elliot and his food—and Max too if he's there."

"You really want me to meet your friends?" I guess Leo really did want me in his life, not just his bed.

"Is that okay?"

I nodded. "Yes. I'm just… This means a lot to me."

Leo pulled me to him and kissed me softly. "*You* mean a lot to me."

"Wow. I think I might swoon."

He chuckled. "I've never been good at the romance part, but with you, I want to try."

In that moment, he could have asked me for absolutely anything, and I would have given it to him. "I wish I'd known we were going out. I would've dressed up too."

Leo shook his head. "I did this for you. Besides, you look hot no matter what you wear."

I was in a worn UNC-Asheville T-shirt and jeans, clothes I'd expected to shuck quickly so Leo could fuck me. "But I'm—"

He kissed me again. "You're perfect."

Heat rushed to my face as I gave him a slow once-over. "No. Tonight, you're perfect. I really like this outfit."

"You think I should dress up more?"

I nodded. "It would be worth it for you, because when you look like that, I want to give you anything you ask for."

He raised his brows. "Anything? Knowing what I like, you'd offer me anything?"

I shrugged. "You know my limits."

"I do, and I was kind of hoping we might press up against some of them this weekend. Not your hard limits, but things you aren't sure about."

I swallowed and licked my lips, loving the sound of that. "Which ones?"

"I'm going to let that be a surprise after I have taken you out, bought you a nice bottle of wine, and fed you some of Elliot's incredible food."

"So you're taking me to dinner with the hopes of wowing me enough that I'll give you what you want?"

Leo grinned. "You just said I could have anything."

"Maybe I was exaggerating."

"Maybe you need a spanking before we go."

I grinned. "Normally, I wouldn't mind that, but I'm really hungry."

Leo rolled his eyes as he reached for my hand. "In that case, we'd better go see Max and Elliot."

Butterflies begin to swirl in my stomach. I was going to meet friends of Leo's who were also friends of my dad. And they knew Leo and I were together.

"Wren, whatever you're thinking about, stop."

"Are you sure Max and Elliot don't think what we're doing is wrong?"

"You mean planning to tell Graham about us tomorrow?"

I shook my head. "No. Us being together."

"They don't. I promise."

Okay. I could do this. "After I meet them, we have to figure out what to say to my dad."

"We'll talk about it over dinner, and then I'll bring you home and wear you out so thoroughly, you won't think about it again until morning."

"I like the sound of that. I really want to enjoy this night with you in case… um… in case it's our last one."

He shook his head as he took my hands in his and squeezed them. "This is not going to be our last night together unless you decide that's what you want. I hope you don't do that, though, because I care about you, and I don't want this to end, not anytime soon, maybe not…"

"Ever?" Could he really mean that? Did he see us together long term? I wanted that so badly. I'd never thought I would, not for a long time anyway, but Leo just felt right to me, like home.

"Does that scare you?" he asked.

I thought for a moment before answering, because it did and it didn't. In a way, being with Leo seemed inevitable, despite my fear. "Not really. No."

"I know you're young and probably not ready to consider what you might want years from now."

"Maybe, but I can't imagine not wanting to be with you."

He smiled at my answer. "All right. Then let's go to dinner."

When we arrived at Contemporary Wine, I saw Lotus on Wheels parked near the patio. Leo raised an arm in greeting to a man with dark, wavy hair who was wearing an amazing vintage suit. He saw Leo and headed our way.

"Max, this is Wren. He's working on his master's in architecture, and I bet he'd love to see your apartment."

Max smiled as he held out his hand for me to shake. "I live close to here in a historic home that was converted to apartments. I have a really interesting loft room, almost like a turret."

"Wow. I would like to see that sometime."

"Maybe Sunday would work. I know you have plans tomorrow with… um…" His cheeks turned pink like maybe he thought he shouldn't mention my dad.

"I know you and my dad are friends."

"Of course. I'm sorry." He looked so flustered; I felt bad for him. "I don't have any problem with you and Leo being together, okay?"

"Thank you."

He glanced toward the food truck. "I know how important it is to act on your feelings, and how happy that can make you."

"Max and Elliot are disgustingly cute together," Leo said.

Max scowled at him. "We're not that bad."

"I'm sure they're not worse than Avery and my dad."

"Exactly," Max said. "No one is worse than them."

We laughed, and I could see why Leo and my dad both liked Max. He was easy to talk to and seemed genuinely interested in what I had to say. We talked for several more minutes, and then he encouraged us to find a table and put our orders in before it got even more crowded.

"Do you want to join us?" Leo asked.

"No, I'm actually heading home to work on some books I found at an estate sale last weekend. I'll be back later when things have settled down."

"Max restores antique books," Leo said.

He really was an interesting man. "That sounds like such a cool job."

"It's just a hobby. My day job is being a bookkeeper; that's actually how I met Leo and your dad."

"I'd like to see some of your books when you show me your building."

"Absolutely. You can get my number from Leo."

"I'll do that. It was great meeting you," I said.

"You too. Have a good evening."

"I like him," I told Leo after Max had walked away.

Leo grinned. "I knew you would." He glanced around. The crowd had grown just since we'd arrived. "If you trust me to order food for you, you can find us a table. I'll put our order in and bring the food when it's ready."

"Sounds good. Just don't get me anything that's crazy spicy."

"I'll keep that in mind."

I found us a seat on the patio. The night was cool, but not cold enough to make sitting outside unpleasant. I had a good view of the food truck, and I quickly became mesmerized watching Elliot chatting with customers at the window.

"You didn't tell me how hot Elliot is," I said when Leo made it to our table.

He huffed. "Elliot's not the one who's going to make you fly tonight."

"That doesn't keep me from looking."

Leo laughed. "He is totally hot, and his food is just as amazing."

Leo ordered us a bottle of wine, which ended up going perfectly with the food. I hadn't thought I really liked wine until I started having monthly family dinners where my dad ordered bottles for the table. I was glad I could truly appreciate Leo's taste. For dinner, Leo had ordered me the bulgogi rice bowl, and he'd gotten himself a spicier version of the same thing with pork instead of beef.

I could barely keep from moaning over my first taste. It was just spicy enough to make my mouth tingle and all the flavors blended together perfectly.

"This is so good. Thank you for sharing it with me."

Leo beamed. "I'm glad you like it, and I want to share everything with you. I don't want to hide anymore."

I laid a hand over his. "After tomorrow, we won't have to." My dad might not be speaking to us, but at least we'd be able to go out anywhere we wanted to.

"So now that we're out as a couple, where else would you like to go?"

I nearly swallowed my wine the wrong way. "A couple? We're a couple?"

"Yes. Unless you don't want to be." Leo actually blushed. I doubted many people could make him do that.

"No, I do. I just didn't expect you to say it."

"I was serious when I said I was thinking about forever. I know that sounds crazy. It's only been a few weeks, but—"

"It's okay. I feel the same way." The smile he gave me was worth any number of embarrassing confessions.

"So tell me where else I should take you," Leo said.

"I intend to take *you* to my favorite dive bar in Asheville and order the bacon-covered dates, because everyone should experience them."

Leo laughed. "I could definitely be into that."

"I also want to go to Succumb and dance with you there, on a night when my dad won't be there, of course."

Leo grimaced. "Yeah. That's going to be a tricky situation, but I would love to dance with you."

We took a break from talking to eat more, and then Leo began telling me about the other dishes he'd had from Elliot's truck. He was far more animated than usual, and I didn't think that was just the wine. I had trouble focusing on what he was saying, because his words faded to the background as I studied his expressions, his bright eyes, cheeks that were flushed from the heat of the food or the wine, the way he used his hands to talk, and those fucking suspenders that I wanted to remove with my teeth.

"Wren? Did you hear me?"

"Oh, sorry. What?"

"I asked if you wanted more wine?" He was holding the bottle near my glass.

"Yes, thank you."

"You're welcome." He was smirking at me.

"You're distracting," I said in my defense. "You're also a closet foodie, aren't you?"

"I like food."

I narrowed my eyes at him. "You like hipster food."

He shrugged. "So what if I do?"

"It just means I'm taking you to tons of hipster places."

"Like ones that serve bacon-wrapped dates?"

"Exactly."

"And lobster nachos?"

I laughed. "Of course."

"There's a place in Asheville that has the absolute best ones."

"Limones?" I asked.

"Yes. I suppose you've been there with Avery and your dad."

I nodded. "Avery is obsessed with the churros."

"They are pretty incredible."

"True." And now I wanted to share some with Leo.

"Maybe you could come to Asheville with me one weekend," he said as if he'd read my mind.

"I'd like that."

"I usually stay in one of your dad's condos, but maybe it's time to find another arrangement."

"Yeah, at least if I'm going to be with you."

Leo reached for my hand and squeezed it. "We'll work it all out."

"But you were looking forward to having more time to hang out with my dad when you were in Asheville."

"Let's not worry about that now, okay?"

I nodded, but no matter what Leo had said earlier, I couldn't help feeling like this might truly be our last night together. If Leo had to choose between me and my dad, shouldn't he choose their long-term friendship?

I realized Leo was giving me his Dom stare. "You're worrying when I told you not to, boy. Do I need to take you to the bathroom and remind you to obey me?"

I nearly choked on my wine.

"Do I?"

"No, Sir."

17

LEO

I was teasing Wren about the plans I had for later tonight, when I heard someone say, "Is that Leo?"

I froze. Fuck, no. It couldn't be.

"Um... I don't think so." That was definitely Avery's voice.

Wren's eyes widened. He'd heard them too.

"Leo, hi, we——"

Graham stopped a few feet from our table. Avery, Sean, and Blake were right behind him. "Wren, what are you doing here?"

Neither Wren nor I said a word. There were plenty of reasonable explanations for Wren being with me, but not one of them came to mind.

Graham looked back and forth between us. "Oh. Wait. No... You're not... Is this why everybody's been acting strange?" He looked at Avery then.

Avery's expression gave it away. And Sean and Blake looked nearly as guilty.

"So you all knew? And none of you bothered to tell me."

"Wren or Leo needed to be the one to tell you," Avery said.

"You could've at least admitted there was something going on with Wren last weekend," Graham snarled. I'd never seen him angry with Avery like that. I was about to tell him to back off when he turned to me. "I didn't even know you and Wren knew each other."

Avery cleared his throat. "I introduced them."

"Avery, what were you thinking?"

Avery didn't back down. In fact, he stood up straighter and took a step toward Graham. "In the moment, I was thinking Wren really needed someone to talk to after a really bad night. Leo's a good listener." Avery's tone was vicious. He was at least as angry as Graham, if not more so.

I glanced at Wren. He'd paled and his eyes were wide. In that moment, I hated myself for coming between him and his family.

"So you didn't intend this to happen?" Graham asked.

Blake stepped forward. "Graham." There was a warning in his tone, but before he could say anything else, Wren pushed back from the table and stood.

"I'm right here, and I'm a fucking adult, so if you have something to say, say it to me."

Graham ignored him, turning to me instead. "Leo, what the fuck?"

"Like Wren just said, he's an adult. Avery called me, and I came to help him."

"I guess this"—he gestured between the two of us—"is why you've been avoiding me."

"I haven't been avoiding you." Not really. Not entirely.

"You haven't called or texted in over a week."

"He said no when I first asked for this," Wren said, his voice loud and angry.

I was thankful for the band that was playing just inside. The music would drown out most of the shouting, but there were still people staring at us.

"He had no idea who I was at first," Wren said. "I made Avery keep it a secret. Then when I confessed, Leo said we couldn't see each other again. He didn't want to jeopardize your friendship or our relationship. But I pushed, because I wanted this. I wanted him."

"My best friend," Graham needlessly pointed out.

"Yes. A man I know I can trust, because you trust him. Someone who will take care of me, who will never hurt me like the guy he and Avery rescued me from."

"What are you talking about? Who hurt you?"

"It doesn't matter now. I'm fine. I called you that night, but you weren't available, and after Avery helped me, I didn't want to say anything. I hadn't even told you I was bi."

Graham looked so hurt that I felt sorry for him. "Wren, you know that would never matter to me. I'd guessed that you might be bi, but I wanted to give you a chance to come to me whenever you were ready."

"I knew you'd be fine with it. I was just waiting for the right time, but why aren't you fine with me being with Leo? Why is it wrong?"

Graham closed his eyes for a moment. His chest rose and fell as he took a slow breath. "Technically, it's not wrong. You're an adult, and Leo is trustworthy, but…" He paused and ran a hand over his hair. "But you're my son, and he… The worst of it is that you kept it from me when everyone else knew. Do you know how stupid that makes me feel?"

"We were trying to give them time to decide how to tell you," Sean said.

Avery nodded. "I told you Wren was worried about a new relationship, but he wasn't ready to talk to you."

"It would've been nice to be told the truth." Graham turned and walked away.

I stood and pulled Wren to me. I was afraid he might push me away, but he wrapped his arm around me and held on tight.

Tears began to run down Avery's cheeks, and Sean hugged him. "It's going to be okay, sweetie. He's going to realize what he's done, and he'll be very sorry."

"I don't think he's really angry with you," I said. "He's just being an idiot."

"I'm so sorry, Avery. I knew Dad would be pissed at me and Leo, but I never thought…"

"It's not your fault." Avery swiped at his tears.

Blake laid a hand on his shoulder. "Why don't we take you back to our hotel, and we'll order some takeout for dinner."

"I… um… okay… but what about Graham? Where will he go?"

Blake frowned. "You and Sean go on back, and I'll look for him, okay?"

"Okay." Avery's voice shook.

I volunteered to help, but Blake shook his head.

"He might talk to me when I find him, but if you're there…"

I hated that the man who'd been more like family to me than anyone else, didn't even want me near him. "You're right."

"Don't worry. I'll do everything I can to make him get his head on straight. I led a SEAL team, I can handle this."

"Thank you."

When he'd walked away, I turned to Wren. He looked

wary and so fucking defeated. I was determined to do anything I could to make the pain in his eyes go away.

"Do you think Avery will be okay?"

I nodded. "I do. Graham is being an asshole right now, but he loves Avery. Blake's right. He's going to realize that and come crawling back to Avery, ready to beg for forgiveness."

Wren glanced toward the parking lot where Sean was tucking Avery into Blake's SUV. "I knew it was selfish to ask you to risk your friendship with Graham, but I never thought I was putting Avery's relationship with my dad at risk."

I took both his hands in mine. "You didn't do anything wrong. All you did was ask for a chance to get what you need. You deserve that as much as your dad or Avery or anyone else."

"But I didn't just ask. I forced you into this."

I shook my head. "No. If you think for one minute I didn't want you from the moment we met, you're way off base."

"The moment we met?"

"Yes, I'm such a fucking pervert that even when you were still scared from what that asshole did to you, I wanted you. Not just because you're hot, I mean you are, but it was the way you reacted to me. Even though you were scared, you still looked at me. I wanted to show you that you could experience erotic pain without ever feeling like a victim. I wanted you to know that you're beautiful and strong and perfect. I wanted to worship you."

His eyes went wide. "You... I..."

"I only like to give pain when it pleases my partner, and what I really want is to take someone as high as they can go and show them how special they are by finding the right way to please them. Most people would think that's crazy, but I've been doing this long enough to know I'm not alone. Most Doms aren't what people imagine when they hear the term."

"It doesn't sound crazy to me. I don't want to be weak, but I want to let go and let pain heighten my pleasure. I used to think that was sick and wrong, but now…"

"It's not wrong at all as long as you're with someone who wants your pleasure."

"I wanted you that night too. At first I was afraid I was just feeling that way about you because you'd been so nice to me or because I was desperate, but that wasn't it. You're special."

I was afraid my voice would crack if I tried to speak again. Graham had been the most important person in my life for a long time. But what I felt for Wren wasn't something I could walk away from. How could I make Graham understand that? He knew how powerful feelings like this could be, because he'd cared for Avery from the very beginning. But I was afraid he would never see it the same way when his son was in the picture.

"If you need some space or you just want to be alone tonight, that's okay. Just tell me what you need."

The look of anguish on Wren's face nearly killed me. "I need you. That's all. Just you."

"That's what I want too."

He looked so relieved. "Good."

"You know how I'd planned to do something to push your limits?"

He nodded.

"I still want that. I want to stretch you out on the bed, tie you down, and hurt you. I want that, because it will feel good to both of us. I want to kiss you, worship you, and hold you afterwards, but I want to hurt you first." I was afraid I'd see horror on his face, but he smiled for the first time since Graham had recognized us.

"I want that too."

"Really?"

He nodded. "I can't think of anything that would make me feel better now than letting you send me into subspace."

"Thank you so much for trusting me to do that for you."

"I trust you with everything."

Nothing could fix what had just happened, but his words came damn close.

18

WREN

Leo fisted the front of my shirt and yanked me into the apartment, shoving the door closed with his other hand. He walked me back until I was pressed against the wall. Then he dragged my hands over my head and pinned them there as he ground against me, kissing me like our lives depended on it. In seconds, he had me achingly hard and desperate for everything I knew he could give me. I wasn't sure what exactly he had in mind for the night, but I knew he would warn me about what was coming if he needed to, so I relaxed back against the wall and let him kiss, nip, and lick my lips... my jaw... my neck. I hadn't thought I'd be able to surrender like that to anyone, but with Leo it felt just right.

For a second, an image flashed in my mind of the hurt and anger on my father's face when he realized Leo and I were together, but I pushed it away. I'd think about that later; I deserved to enjoy my time with Leo first.

Leo let go of my hands and reached for my hips instead. Then he turned me around, so I was facing the wall. "Brace yourself and stick your ass out."

I did as he said, and he unfastened my pants and shoved them and my briefs down my legs. He gripped my ass cheeks, squeezing hard. I sucked in my breath and arched my back, pushing into his rough touch.

He brought his hand down across my ass, and I wiggled it, wanting more. He obliged me. The blows weren't particularly hard, but they were enough to warm and redden my skin. I hoped he was enjoying the sight. When he stopped, I glanced over my shoulder and saw him sink to his knees.

"Oh, God, Leo, are you…" I felt his warm breath against my skin.

"Going to eat your ass? Yes, I am."

"Fuck. I've never…" He licked me from my taint to the base of my spine, making me gasp.

"Are you saying you've never been rimmed before?"

"Yeah." It was all I could do to get the single word out with him blowing against my hole. "Please." I held myself still, even though I wanted to move. I didn't want to do anything to risk him changing his mind.

"Don't worry, boy. I'll give you what you want."

I whimpered as his tongue teased my entrance.

"Like that, boy?"

"Y-yes, Sir."

"Want me to fuck that pretty hole with my tongue?"

"Please! Yes!"

He chuckled against me, and I felt the vibrations along my skin. He made me wait until my legs were trembling, and then he pushed the tip of his tongue into me. The sensation was amazing, even better than I'd imagined. He teased me, circling my rim and shifting his attention to my balls. When he pushed in again, I cried out. This time he fucked me deeper and faster. He was so damn good at this. It was warm and wet, and I couldn't stay still. I squirmed and pushed back, trying to get more, but Leo gripped my hips tightly, keeping me from moving like I wanted to.

I could easily come from what he was doing. I wouldn't even need to touch myself. "Leo? I don't know if I can hold back if you—"

He sat back on his heels.

"No," I whined. "I didn't mean you should stop."

He smacked my ass, harder than he had before. "I'm not ready for you to come yet, boy, not even close." He stood and leaned against me, pressing me into the wall. Then he whispered right by my ear. "We've got some things to talk through, because I want to do things to you that might push your limits."

He stood up and encouraged me to turn and face him, so I did.

"I need to know if you're okay with that. If not, we'll find something else to do. There's no pressure. You understand that, boy?"

I nodded. "Yes, Sir."

"Come sit on the bed." He took my hand and led me to the bedroom. I tried to ignore the throbbing of my cock and the heat from where he'd spanked me, but that seemed impossible.

When I sat down, he knelt in front of me, placing his hands on my thighs. I opened my legs, so he could fit between them. I could tell he was nervous. Maybe some people wouldn't see it, but I did.

I smiled, trying to reassure him. "You can ask me for anything."

"I want to try needle play with you."

I sucked in my breath, feeling a little scared but a lot turned on. I was in the mood for him to push me.

"Before you decide how you feel about this, I want you to know I've had training, not just from other people in the

BDSM community, but also from a professional piercer. I'm certified to do piercings, but nothing I do today will be staying in place, and the needles will be much thinner than the ones used for most piercings."

I shivered a bit as I imagined him piercing me for real, putting rings in me, ones that would stay. "I want to try it."

Leo smiled. "Thank you. I'll start with a less intense area, and we'll work up to more. Before I use any of the needles, we'll do some sensation play with ice, a crop, maybe other things that are familiar. I have everything we need to be safe: gloves, alcohol pads, absorbent pads for the bed. The needles are medical grade, and they're brand-new. I'll show you the package before I open them."

I took hold of his hands and squeezed them. "You already know I trust you."

"Trusting me to spank you or restrain you is different than this. This can truly be dangerous. I want you to know I've done this before, and I know how to anticipate emergencies that could arise. What do you think?"

"I still think yes."

He rose up a bit so he could give me a gentle kiss. "I'm going to do everything I can to make this good for you, but there's no pressure for you to like it, okay?"

I nodded. "Okay."

"Lie down, and I'll get everything we need."

19

LEO

I stepped into my en suite bathroom and opened the cabinet where I'd placed the supplies I'd ordered when I realized Wren might be willing to try one of my favorite things. I pulled out a box of surgical gloves and the needles I'd chosen—some of the thinnest ones used for play. I also grabbed first aid supplies, lube, and a condom. I'd already put some waterproof pads on the bed just in case there was any blood, though usually there was no more than the tiniest drop when the needles were taken out.

When I stepped back into the bedroom, Wren was lying on his back looking very nervous, which I had to admit turned me on. I knew his nerves were mixed with excitement and anticipation. I was more touched than I could express that he trusted me enough to try this for me.

His eyes widened when he saw all the supplies in my hands. I set them down on the bench at the end of the bed. "I'll be right back. I just need to get a few more things."

"Wow. You really had to do a lot of planning for this."

I smiled. "That's part of being a good Dom." I got the last few things we needed, including a bowl of ice, my favorite riding crop, a cock ring, and a blindfold. Some subs enjoyed watching the needles go in, or it might be best to say they enjoyed *hating* watching the needles go in. Others preferred to be blindfolded, because not knowing what would happen could be a huge turn-on or because while they could handle the pain, the sight of the needles piercing their skin was too much. I would let Wren decide what worked for him.

"I'm going to restrain your wrists and ankles like I did for electricity play," I told him when I returned to the bedroom. "Like I said before, we'll start with sensation play. I'd like to blindfold you for that so you don't know exactly what's coming next. Is that all right?"

"Yes. I like not knowing."

"Good. When we start with needle play, you can ask me to remove the blindfold if you want to see, or you can leave it on."

"I think I'll want to leave it on."

"That's fine, but you can change your mind any time. Now reach your arms above your head and stretch out your legs." Once I had his restraints in place, I put a cock ring on him. I intended to give him a hell of a lot of stimulation, but he wasn't going to come until we finished with our pain play.

I ran my hand over his chest, caressing him. Once he seemed relaxed, I pinched his nipples hard. He arched up, gasping. I loved how sensitive he was there. I teased the hard buds a little more, thinking how, if things went well, I'd be sticking needles through them later, hearing him cry out, watching him writhe as he tried to deal with the pain.

I picked up the crop and started to warm him up with it, giving light taps to his thighs, his pecs, his arms, then his cock, his balls, and his already stimulated nipples. I loved the way he squirmed, seeming to be unsure whether to reach for the blows or try to get away from them.

After a while, I squirted some lube in one hand and began stroking his cock as I alternated between his thighs and his nipples with the crop. Soon he was working his hips to try and get more friction.

"More, Leo, please."

I let him go, laid down the crop, and picked up a piece of ice in each hand. When I pressed the ice to each of his nipples, he cried out, twisting and begging. I drew the ice down over his abdomen, then held it to his balls. My hands ached from the cold, but it was so worth it to hear him whimper.

"It's too cold, Leo. Fuck. Please. I can't take it."

"You can do this. I know you can. I love that you're willing to suffer for me."

He groaned. "I didn't think ice would be so intense."

I loved how many new experiences I was able to give him. "It can be, if it's used right." I grabbed another piece and pressed it against his hole.

"Jesus!"

I teased him with it, pushing it into him as it melted. He twisted on the bed, trying to pull away from my hand.

"I love how fucking responsive you are and how hard your cock is, despite you struggling to take this."

"I... Thank you," he said between pants.

I dropped all the ice back into the bowl and dried my hands on a towel.

"Are you ready for more?"

He shivered. "Yes. I think so. Yes."

I lifted the edge of the blindfold, so he could see me. "You don't have to do this."

"I know. I want to."

I felt better seeing his eyes as he said it. "Do you want to keep the blindfold on?"

He considered my question for a few seconds. "Part of me wants to see the needles, but... I don't think I can watch you put them in. Maybe I can look afterwards."

"That's absolutely fine. I would love for you to see yourself all decorated, but if you don't want to do that either, that's fine, and we may not even get as far as I'm thinking."

Wren licked his lips. "How far would that be?"

"I'd like for that to be a surprise. I think that it will be easier if we work up to it instead of you worrying about what might happen."

He nodded. "So with a blindfold on, I'll have no idea where the needles are going?"

"Not exactly. I have to pinch the skin and then stretch it a bit before sliding a needle in. You understand these needles go across the skin so they're just sliding through the top few layers like a piercing, not stabbing into you like a shot."

"Yeah, I... um... I watched some videos after we talked about it the first time. They were... um... intense."

I cupped his face and brushed my thumb over his cheekbone. "You're going to do beautifully. I know you are."

"Thank you, Sir."

I pulled the blindfold back down. "If you change your mind and you want it off, just say yellow."

"Yes, Sir."

"I may return to ice or the crop at some point to mix up the sensations or to give you a different kind of pain."

He drew in his breath. "Whatever you think best; just please go ahead and start. The anticipation is killing me."

"That's part of the fun," I said as I pulled on gloves and got everything ready.

I teased him at first, pinching him on his abdomen, his pecs, his arms. He tensed when I pinched his nipples. Not wanting him too scared, I said, "We won't start there."

"S-start?"

"That's right."

"But you might…"

"We'll see."

I opened the first needle and pinched the skin along the top of his thigh, an area that was usually easy for subs to handle. A few seconds later, I slid the first needle in.

He squirmed and bit his lip like he was trying to hold in a cry, but he relaxed again quickly.

"You did good, boy. Are you okay?"

"Yeah. It's not so bad. More just sensation now, not really pain."

"That's how it should be. I'm going to keep going, okay?"

"Yes, please."

Those words meant so much to me. I loved that we could share this. "Don't hold back. I want to hear how it feels, but try to stay still."

I inserted five more needles, two more in the same leg and three in the other. His breath caught with each one, but he barely moved.

After the last one, I bent and kissed a line down his abdomen, coming close to the head of his cock but not touching it. He arched up just a little, reaching for my mouth. I smiled against his skin. "Hungry for more?"

"God, yes. Leo, I think I like this."

"Really?"

"Yes, it's a little scary, and I feel so vulnerable, but I love how the needles make me so… aware of the skin where they are. I'm so fucking hard right now. I know you can see that, but…"

I glanced down at his cock which was leaking precum onto his abdomen. "Yes, I can."

I picked up a piece of ice and slid it over his shaft. He cried out even as he bucked up, trying to get friction. I ran the ice over his balls and then up his abdomen and chest, loving how he squirmed and protested.

Now I had to decide where the next needle was going. Was he ready for one in his cock?

20

WREN

I shivered. Cold water droplets slid down my chest, and Leo was making me wait now, not giving any hint what was coming next. The crop? More needles? Where would the next ones go? My nipples tightened at the thought of him putting them there. Could I stand that? Scary as it was, I wanted to find out.

"Leo?"

"Yes, boy?"

"I think…" I paused to swallow. "I think I can take something more intense."

"Good, because that's what I want to give you."

"Wh-where are the next needles going?"

"Wherever I want them to."

"Fuck." I hated how much my body liked that answer.

He chuckled. The sound was warm, but it made me shiver anyway. I drew in a shaky breath as I waited for him to touch me again.

Finally, he began tugging at the skin along my shaft. Was he really going to put one there? I braced myself as he bent and ran his tongue up my cock. The pleasure was as intense as the pain I expected the needles to cause.

He pinched my shaft again, tugging on the skin.

"Sir?"

"Yes, boy?"

"Are you really going to put a needle there?"

"Do you want me to?"

I thought for a moment, not sure whether I could voice that desire. I was afraid of this pain in a way I hadn't been afraid of the other things he'd done to me. Could I actually want him to put a needle in my dick? Was that crazy?

"I want you to be honest with me either way," he said.

"I do want you to. I want to know what it feels like and whether I can take it. I want to give this to you."

"Then relax. If you're too tense, I risk hurting you in a way I don't mean to." He laid his hand on my chest. "Take a deep breath and push my hand up."

I did as he said, filling my lungs as full as I could.

"Good boy. Now let it out slowly."

I started to exhale.

"Let your body sink into the mattress. Just let go and relax." I did, and that's when he stuck the needle in near the base of my cock. The sting was so intense it took my breath. I gave a high-pitched cry and jerked, trying to pull away. But the needle wasn't going anywhere.

"Fuck. Fuck. Fuck." It had hurt like hell, but the pain was already fading, leaving me with that odd sensation of awareness.

"Shh, baby, it's okay." Leo rubbed my side, trying to soothe me.

He wrapped his other hand around my cock and stroked me. I worked my hips, fucking his hand, needing more, so much more. Pleasure quickly overtook the last residual pain. I was ready to beg him to fuck me, when he let go and pinched a small bit of skin higher up on my shaft.

Oh, God, I wasn't sure I could take this again.

"Deep breath," Leo said.

I tried to breathe, but my body tensed, knowing what was coming. "I... I can't."

"Do you need me to stop?"

If we stopped, I would have given Leo more than he likely expected, but I didn't really want to stop. I liked how it hurt, liked how it scared me. I just needed to be pushed. I'd survived having a needle through the skin of my dick. I could do more, right?

"No. I don't want to stop." I was able to take a deep breath then and let it out slowly. I expected Leo to push the needle through, but he didn't.

I knew he had one in his hand. I'd heard him open it. He liked making me wait, catching me off guard. *Relax*, I told myself as I took another breath. I'd just started to exhale when he pushed it in. I screamed again. There was no way to stop the sound. It hurt, and it scared me. Suddenly, I needed the blindfold gone. I needed to see what I'd done, what I'd allowed Leo to do to me.

"Yellow. Blindfold off. Please."

Leo pushed it off right away. I looked down at the needles he'd pierced me with. I'd thought it might scare me to see them and wondered if I'd beg him to put the blindfold back on. Instead, I was fascinated. The needles looked amazing.

"Wow. That's fucking hot."

Leo grinned. "Damn right it is."

"I think I want to watch the next one. Unless... are you done?"

"Only if you need me to be."

I looked down again, studying the needles running

through my cock. "I don't. Are you going to put more between those two?"

Leo shook his head. "Not today. I want to start slow. But another time, I'd like to do a whole row." He ran his finger along my cock between the two needles. "And then I'd like to take the violet wand and run it along them, letting the metal intensify the current."

I shuddered, trying to imagine how that would feel. "That would be... wow."

"I think so too."

Leo gripped my cock and stroked it, sliding his hand between the two needles but keeping his touch far lighter than what I craved. I told myself not to react, not to push into his hand, but my hips moved of their own volition. A few seconds later, Leo let go.

"So... um... where do you want to put the other needles?"

Leo grinned as he flicked his thumbs over my nipples.

"Oh, fuck."

"Oh, yes." He pinched them lightly at first and then harder, rolling them between his thumbs and forefingers.

This was really going to hurt. My nipples were particularly sensitive, or at least they seemed to be compared to the other guys I'd been with. This might hurt more than the ones on my cock.

"What do you think?" Leo asked. "Should we try it?"

I needed to know how it felt. I needed to know if the pain would be as delicious as I imagined, but it was still hard to ask for something like that.

"Wren? Are you okay?" Leo stroked my side, and I looked up, meeting his gaze.

"I'm fine. I'm just nervous, and it's hard to ask. It's... um... easier when you force me, force me with my consent, I mean."

Leo nodded. "I understand. Are you nervous because of how much it will hurt? Or nervous because you're not sure you want it?"

His obvious concern for me made it easier to respond. "The first one."

"Okay, and you want to watch?"

I hesitated for a second. "I think so."

"I'll leave the blindfold off for now. Just use your safeword if you decide you don't want to see what I'm doing, and I'll stop, even if I've got the needle ready to go in."

"Okay. That's… that's fine."

He studied me for a moment. "I think you need the crop first."

The familiarity of that pain would make it easier. "Yes, please."

He picked it up, and I closed my eyes. I wanted to watch him with the needles, but being cropped was better when I didn't know where the blows would land.

He slapped my thighs, my upper arms, the soles of my feet. The blows were just hard enough to get my attention. Leo was forcing me to focus on sensation, instead of on my fear of the pain.

He surprised me by smacking my cock right between the needles. "So good!" I cried out as I bucked up, gasping.

"You're incredible." I could hear awe in Leo's voice.

He returned his attention to less sensitive areas. Then, without warning, he cropped one of my nipples. Before I'd recovered, he slapped the other one and continued to move back and forth between them until I was begging him to stop.

"Look at me," he ordered when he finally did.

I did, gazing into his dark eyes.

"Tell me how it feels."

"It fucking hurts," I said, feeling angry and desperate, not sure I could take the needles now that I was so sore.

"I know, baby, but if you can take the crop, you can take the needles."

"But now I'm already sore, and—"

"You're already stimulated and aware, so you'll focus even more when I slide the needle through here." He tugged on one of my nipples.

"You're a bastard."

Leo chuckled. "I'm just giving you what you asked for."

"Fuck you."

Leo slapped my thigh with the crop, making me yelp. "You definitely need to work on the submission part of this."

"You just fucking stabbed my cock."

He cropped me again, hard.

"Fuck! I'm sorry, Sir."

"Damn right you should be."

I looked up, wanting him to see the desperation in my eyes. "Please don't stop."

Leo smiled at me. "I have no intention of stopping. I'm looking forward to your reaction when I push more needles into you. Your nipples are so delightfully sensitive."

"Oh, God."

Leo grinned as he pulled on a new pair of gloves and reached for the package of needles.

I tensed. Could I really watch this?

He pinched my nipple and then tugged on it, stretching it. He held a needle in one hand.

"I… I don't…"

"You can take this, boy. I know you can."

He brought the needle closer.

"Oh, fuck no."

"Do you remember your safeword, boy?"

I nodded. "Don't need it."

I didn't want to stop this, and I could always close my eyes if I decided I couldn't watch. The needle was so close now. Leo teased my nipple, rubbing the tip and then running his nails over it. Then he pinched hard and—holy fucking fuck—pushed the needle in. I keened, the sound horrible. I hadn't meant to fight him, but I did, writhing and yanking on my restraints. "No. Please. No!"

It seemed as if time slowed. It took forever for him to send the needle all the way through the puckered tip. The pain eased once it was in, and I realized Leo was smiling. He looked so pleased. I glanced at my nipple. "Fuck, you really did it?"

He nodded. "I did, and you took it beautifully, boy."

"But I—"

He shook his head. "You were wonderful. Let's do the other one."

"Th-the other one?"

He grinned. "You wouldn't want to leave the other side all bare, would you?"

"You're evil."

"And you love it."

"Yeah. I do."

Leo opened another package and pulled out a new needle. This time he didn't tease me, he just pinched and tugged and then the needle was there almost before I realized it. I tensed, trying to make myself watch, but I closed my eyes just as the pain hit, and I gasped. All the air seemed to leave me as I struggled, fighting the intensity of the sensation.

"Breathe, baby," Leo said. "It's over now."

I was finally able to suck in air and let it whoosh back out.

"That's it. Just relax and breathe."

I took a few deeper breaths, and then I looked. There really were needles through both my nipples. I'd actually done this.

"I'm so proud of you, boy. I didn't think we'd get this far today." The look on Leo's face as he glanced from one pierced nipple to the other and then down at my cock sent heat racing through my body. As the stinging pain in my nipples lessened, the endorphins seemed to channel right into sexual need. My cock ached, and I felt restless. I needed to be fucked.

"Is that all we're doing?" I asked.

"With needles? Yes. I'm not going to push you any further today." He gave a light tap to the needle in my right nipple. A confusing mix of pain and pleasure jolted me as more precum dripped onto my stomach.

"Please," I begged.

"Please do that again?" He tapped the needle on the other side, and I groaned.

"No. Please. Need you. Need you to fuck me."

"That's exactly what I'm going to do. I'm going to take your ass with these needles in you. I'm going to love watching you writhe and beg while you're all decorated for me."

"Yes. Please. I want that."

Leo stripped off his gloves, tossed them into a plastic container, and released my ankle restraints. He rolled on a condom while I flexed my feet and worked out the stiffness in my legs.

"I want to fuck you with no prep," he said as he slicked himself up.

"Oh, God. I… I love that."

He smiled as he slicked up his cock. I was so ready to feel him pushing into my ass, but he pulled on a new set of gloves first. "I'm just making sure I'm prepared if I want to touch your cock or your nipples," he explained.

"Oh, right." I'd forgotten he'd need gloves for that, both because there could be blood and the punctures needed to stay clean.

Finally, he took hold of his cock and pushed into me. I wrapped my legs around his waist, trying to keep him there, even though the stretch burned and the jostling of the needles in my thighs made me hiss. By the time he was balls-deep in me, I was panting.

He paused, and I looked up at him.

"Thank you for trusting me to do this," he said.

"I wouldn't have let anyone else try something like this, but it's different with you. I—" Shit. I'd almost said I love you. That was crazy. I couldn't say those words this soon. "I love what you do to me." That would have to be enough for now.

"You're perfect," he said as he pulled out slowly. Then he drove back in. He kept a steady rhythm, not slow, but not fast enough to truly satisfy me. I wrapped my legs around him and pushed against his ass with my heels, trying to get him to go faster.

"You want more?" he asked.

"Yes. Please. I need—"

He drove into me and the movement made my cock bounce, pain and pleasure surging along my shaft from the places where the needles pierced it.

He kept pounding into me and in no time, I was right at the edge. Then, as if he knew that, he paused.

I whined, but he just chuckled and reached over my head to release my wrists. "Hold out your right hand," he ordered.

I didn't know what he wanted, but I obeyed anyway.

He tugged a glove onto my hand and then squirted lube into my palm.

"Jack yourself off, but only touch your cock between the needles. You don't want to rub over them."

"Yes, Sir."

When I wrapped a hand around my cock, a jolt of heat shot through me. I knew I would come in no time. Leo released my cock ring and started pounding into me, fucking me hard enough to push me across the mattress.

"Please," I begged. "Don't stop."

He reached up and tapped one of the needles in my nipples. That was all I needed. I cried out, arching my back as I came. Cum shot across my chest, and Leo put his hand over mine on my cock, helping me stroke myself. The needles intensified everything, and my orgasm felt like it lasted forever. Finally, I collapsed back against the mattress, spent and utterly happy.

Leo drove into me again, and I gasped. It still felt so good, even though I'd just come.

"Fuck me, Leo. I want to see you come. I need... need to know I pleased you."

"Boy, everything about you pleases me." A few seconds later, he stiffened and called out my name as his own orgasm overtook him.

When he'd caught his breath, Leo pulled out of my ass and dropped the condom and gloves into the plastic box where he'd discarded his other gloves. "I need to take the needles out now, boy. It's best to do it while you're still sex drunk."

Oh, shit. I'd forgotten that part.

"I'll go as quickly as I can, okay?"

"Y-yes, Sir."

"You'll be fine. It shouldn't hurt too much."

He removed the ones in my thighs first, dropping them

into the container. Then he took hold of the two in my cock and slid them out at the same time. I hissed. It hurt, but not as much as I'd expected. I glanced down and saw only a tiny drop of blood at one of the openings. Leo dabbed at it with an alcohol pad.

"Fuck. That hurts worse than taking it out."

He chuckled. "Hush, boy, and let me get the last ones out."

I dreaded those most.

"Inhale," he ordered.

As I did, he pulled out both the needles in my nipples. I bit my lip, but a muffled cry came through.

"It's all done now, baby, and I'm so very proud of you. You took so much, and it was only your first time."

I loved that I'd been able to do this for him. "I liked it more than I thought I would."

Leo's smile never left his face as he finished up with aftercare, putting some antibacterial ointment on all the places where he'd put the needles, then discarding everything and bringing me apple juice and a chocolate bar. He tossed the pads he'd put under me and then climbed in bed with me and held me while I ate.

"Is that what it's like to have your nipples pierced?" I asked after I finished the chocolate.

Leo seemed to consider the answer. "Well, those were twenty-two-gauge needles, and I would pierce them with fourteen gauge. The lower the number, the thicker the needle, so—"

"Oh, fuck."

Leo smiled. "I'd love to pierce you for real, boy. I'd put some rings on you that I could tug on. And I could decorate the edges with more needles and send electricity through them."

"My birthday's coming up in a few weeks—November

second. Maybe that would be the perfect present." Oh fuck, what was I saying? If the needles he used today hurt, what would thicker ones feel like?

His eyes widened. "You'd really allow me to…"

I nodded.

"Wren, I… I don't know what to say."

"You told me you were a certified piercer. And I'd already been thinking about getting my nipples pierced, so… um… unless I think too much about those thick needles and get too scared, then… yes, I'd let you." I didn't think I'd ever seen him smile so brightly.

"Wow. We need to talk about this when you're not coming down from a scene, obviously, but if you still want to later, I'd be honored to do it."

"It would be so much more special for you to be the one to pierce me instead of a stranger."

Leo pulled me more tightly against him. "Everything we do is special, Wren. You're like a gift to me."

Heat filled my face. "I… I don't—"

"Shhh. Just let me hold you."

I snuggled against him, and even remembering my dad's reaction at the restaurant didn't lessen how happy I was in that moment.

21

LEO

A knock on the door, more of a pounding really, woke me the next day.

Wren managed to get up first. He pulled on his underwear, stumbled toward the door, and came racing back a few seconds later. "It's my dad."

"Fuck." I grabbed a pair of pants from the laundry and yanked them on.

Wren was still standing there, so I gestured to his clothes on the floor. "Get dressed."

"I was going to hide in here."

I shook my head. "He chose to come here. We told him we were together, so there's no reason to hide."

"All right, but you better get the door."

Graham knocked again, and I pulled a T-shirt on. Wren was stepping into his pants as I headed toward the front door.

When I opened the door, Graham looked at his feet rather than at me. "Is Wren here?"

"Yes. He'll be out in a minute."

"I want to talk to you, or well, I really don't, but Avery

says that's not an option, and I know he's right, goddammit. Do you have any idea how hard this is for me?"

I sighed. "Do you want to talk to both of us or just me?"

I heard Wren's footsteps, and Graham glanced over my shoulder, then back at me. "Both, but maybe not at the same time."

"Fair enough, but before I invite you in, I need to know that this is going to be a civil conversation."

Graham blew out a breath. "I didn't come here to yell at you or tell you you're wrong or whatever. I just want to talk."

"So you don't think what we're doing is wrong?" Wren asked.

"I didn't say that, but—"

I held up a hand. "Give me a minute before we get into anything else." I stepped back and gestured for Graham to come in. Then I closed the door and turned to Wren. "I don't want you to feel like I'm kicking you out, but how do you feel about letting me talk to Graham for a while on my own? I'll call you as soon as we're done."

Wren looked at his dad and then back at me. "That's… fine. I know the two of you need to talk. I'll get my coat and stuff and go."

Graham laid a hand on Wren's arm as he walked by. "I want to talk to you later. I'm sorry for the way I acted last night. I'm not saying I'm completely okay with it, but I should've listened to you."

Wren rubbed his eyes, which were wet with tears. "Thank you for saying that. I didn't mean to hurt you. We should have told you sooner. I didn't want you to find out like you did."

He grabbed his coat from the hall closet and his

computer bag from where it was sitting on the kitchen table.

I wanted to kiss him goodbye, but that was probably not a good idea. Instead, I took his hand and squeezed it. "I'll call you soon, okay?"

He nodded, and I let him go. He slipped out the door and closed it gently behind himself, like he was trying not to make a sound.

Graham and I stared at each other for a few moments. I was the first one to break the silence. "I don't want to lose your friendship or come between you and your son, but I'm not giving him up."

Graham shook his head. "I've always trusted you. Since right after we met. You've been my best friend for eight years, and I never thought... He's my son, Leo. We'd finally figured out how to talk to each other, and now..."

I'd lain in bed the night before planning what to say to Graham when he was ready to talk, but now I couldn't remember any of it. Even if I could, I wasn't sure he'd listen. He was protective of his children, and I understood that. If, after all the time he'd known me, he thought I'd be reckless with his son, what could I possibly say to convince him otherwise?

"Do you really have nothing to say to me?" Graham asked.

"I have a lot to say, but I'm not sure you want to hear any of it."

"An apology would be nice."

"I'm sorry for hiding this from you. We should've told you after the first time we went out."

"But you're not sorry that you're fucking my son?" He sounded so bitter, so angry, not at all like the Graham I knew. It hurt, and I wanted to hurt him back, but I forced myself to breathe for a moment before I spoke.

"Graham, he's twenty-two years old."

"I don't give a fuck how old he is. He's…"

"Old enough to make his own decisions. Did you really think he's never—" Graham held up his hand, and I knew I was about to cross a line, so I stopped. "I shouldn't have to apologize for wanting him."

Graham huffed. "He's too young for you."

I stared at him. "Seriously. That's what you're going with?"

He looked disgusted. With me? With himself? I had no idea. "Fine. I know I can't say shit about the age difference. But I… This is fucking hard for me. You and I were… You fucked me, Leo, and now you're fucking my son."

"I know, but we agreed we weren't right for each other, and it's been years since…"

"That doesn't make it any less fucked up!"

"Graham, I never wanted to hurt you."

He scowled at me. "You should've thought more about that before taking my son to bed."

"Graham, are you really going to walk away from our friendship because your grown-up son and I have a consensual relationship?"

He turned away and wiped at his eyes. Fuck, was he crying? I said, "I didn't mean for this to happen. You know that, right?"

"But I know what you like, Leo. I've seen you do demos with your subs. How am I supposed to be okay thinking about my son being one of those boys?"

I glared at him. "So your support for safe, sane, consensual BDSM and no kink shaming goes out the window when it's a member of your family?"

"Fuck you," Graham snarled.

"Because I'm right."

"This isn't about—"

"What is it about?"

"I trusted you, and you hid this from me," Graham shouted.

At least that accusation was fair. "We were going to tell you tomorrow when we met for brunch. Wren was going to meet us there. We had it all planned."

His eyes widened. "You did? Really?"

"Yes. Did you think we planned to keep it a secret forever? Look, I'm sorry, okay, and I know it's not easy thinking about us being together, knowing what you know about me."

He ran a hand through his hair and sighed. "It's going to be awkward as fuck."

"Going to be? So you're not going to stop talking to me?"

He shook his head. "Fuck, no, Leo. How could I do that?"

Thank God, at least now I had hope.

"Avery says I'm being an ass."

I grinned. "No comment."

"Fine. I am, and I'm not sure I'm ready to stop being one. It might take me a while."

I nodded. "I can wait. You mean a lot to me."

"I'm sorry, I just…"

I shook my head. "I'm fine. But you really need to talk to Wren. I doubt he'll ever say this, but you're breaking his heart."

"Shit. I was just trying to…"

"Protect him?"

"Yes." I knew it was instinctive, but it still hurt.

"You do remember how seriously I take consent, right? He doesn't need protection from me."

"It's not… He's young, and… I know you're safe, but you still do edge play, and—"

"Do you want him to do that with someone else? Someone who might not care as much about safety as me?"

Graham sank onto the couch, looking completely worn out. I wondered if he'd slept much the night before. "I don't fucking know what I want."

"As long as you don't expect Wren to ignore what he wants. Do you remember what it felt like to do that?"

He scowled at me. "Why do you have to be so fucking right?"

I smiled for the first time since he'd gotten there. "I'm just that good."

He rolled his eyes.

I sat down next to him. "I love him, Graham."

"You what?"

"Remember how I told you I'd given up on finding someone I thought I could build a life with?"

Graham nodded slowly.

"Well, I was wrong. I think Wren is that person."

"You're serious? You're in love with Wren?"

"Like you with Avery. That's why I couldn't just walk away from him. I tried, and we were both miserable. I wouldn't have ever considered being with your son if there wasn't more than lust there."

He truly looked stunned. "I don't know what to say. I've hoped you'd find someone who made you feel like I feel about Avery, but I never… I wouldn't have… You've been there for me through so much. I should be able to be happy for you and for Wren, but it's just going to take some time, okay?"

At least he wasn't shutting me out. That was enough for now. "Take the time you need. But I hope eventually, things can be like they were between us or close to it."

Graham nodded. "Me too."

"Before you go, I have to ask you one thing, because no matter what we're working through, I'm not above kicking your ass if I need to. Are things okay with Avery?"

"It took me about an hour to realize how badly I'd fucked up. I groveled a lot and then stayed up most of the night, making sure my boy knows how much I love him."

I grinned at him. "Good. That's all I needed to know."

"I'm going to go see Wren now. I'm anxious to talk to him."

"If he's not home, you should look for him at Ludlow Park. He likes to go there for walks or just to sit and think and people-watch."

"Thanks. That's good to know."

"Call me when you're ready to talk again."

Graham nodded. Then he walked out the door. I really hoped it wouldn't take him too long to come to terms with my relationship with Wren.

22

WREN

I heard leaves rustling and looked up to see my dad walking toward me. Leo must have told him he might find me here.

When Dad reached the bench, he gestured to the seat beside me. "May I join you?"

I was suddenly taken back to two years earlier when he'd found me in a different park, one on the UNC-Asheville campus, and said those same words. That day we'd spoken more than we had in years. It was the start of us growing close again. And now...

I nodded, not sure I could trust my voice.

"I don't want to lose you again," my dad said after he was seated.

"I don't want that either, but I'm not going to break up with Leo just because you don't approve."

"Wren, I—"

I held up my hand. "Do you have any objections that aren't hypocritical?'

After a few moments of looking really determined, he sighed and said, "No."

I tried to hold back my laugh, but I couldn't. "Do you pout like that for Avery?"

"I'm not pouting."

I raised my brows, and he scowled.

"I'm worried about you."

"Why? Because things have gotten serious fast? Because he's older? Because I'm a submissive?"

He grimaced. "I don't—"

"Seriously, Dad? Aren't you the one who's all about the sex-positive attitude?"

"Fuck, yes. I know I'm being a hypocrite. Avery's already told me. And Leo too."

I nodded. "You are, and you were awful to Avery last night."

"Leo's already taken me to task for that and so have Blake and Sean. Trust me. I groveled. A lot."

"Good."

He studied me for a moment. "When you say things are happening fast, what do you mean?"

"I'm in love with him. At least I think I am. Maybe that's crazy, but I can't walk away from him. I care too much."

My dad smiled then, and the tightness in my chest gave way. I could finally breathe again. "I hadn't realized... I guess I didn't give either of you a chance to explain."

"No, you didn't. How were things when you and Leo talked?"

He blew out a harsh breath. "Hard at first and then better. I told him it was going to take me some time to come to terms with your relationship with him, but that I didn't want to lose him."

"He doesn't want to lose you either. That was his main objection to us being together."

My dad nodded.

"So you think you could eventually accept what's between us?"

"I want to."

I shifted, pulling one foot up on the bench and turning to face him. "Good, because it's not going away anytime soon, not if I get my way."

"I'm sure you're determined to do just that."

"Damn right, I am."

"I think Leo is fairly determined too."

"Yeah?" I hadn't really dared to hope Leo felt as strongly as I did. "What did he say?"

"Basically the same thing you just did."

"That this won't end soon?"

"No, that he's in love with you."

I sputtered, and I would've fallen off the bench if my dad hadn't grabbed my arm. "He said that? He actually…"

"Oh, shit. I shouldn't have said that, not when you haven't talked to each other, but—"

"No, it's great. I'm glad you did, because I didn't think… Oh my God… He really…"

My dad laid his hand on my arm. "Take a breath."

I did, and when I'd managed to calm down a little, my dad said, "Are you going to tell Leo I told you?"

"No. Definitely not. I just won't have to be afraid to say it myself."

Dad smiled. "I think he would welcome that."

"Are you saying you're okay with me being in love with him?"

"The whole thing is weird for me. It changes my relationship with Leo, and I've got to figure out how to make that work. But I'm determined to, because I know how powerful love can be. If you both feel that way about each other, then you should be together. Leo's a good man, and

I know he won't hurt you." My dad's cheeks got red, and he coughed a bit. "I mean he won't hurt you more than… Fuck, this is way too awkward."

I couldn't help but laugh. "You're going to have to get over it. I know you know what Leo likes."

He winced. "Can we please not go there?"

"You're the one who brought it up."

"Jesus, I was just… just trying to… I know he won't hurt you in any way you don't want to be hurt, okay?"

"Okay. And I know I'm never going to be able to go to Succumb anytime you and Avery are in town."

My dad shook his head. "No, it's all yours. I… I don't think I could risk it."

"Leo thinks we should do something mature like make up a schedule, but I just think maybe I'm okay at home."

My dad laughed then, his embarrassment seeming to fade. "This really is going to take some adjustment, but I love you, and I'm not going to be a hypocrite and tell you that anything you and Leo do is wrong. As long as you're with someone who respects you and keeps you safe, that's enough. I just wish…"

"That I hadn't fallen for your best friend."

He groaned. "Yes."

"Do you also wish I didn't like what Leo does?"

"No!"

I was surprised by his vehemence.

"As much as I wish I knew fewer details about Leo's preferences and now yours, I would never want to change you like that. I would never ask you to ignore those desires, either. I know how awful that feels, because I did it for years."

I frowned. "But instead of trying to understand how hard that was for you, I treated you like shit."

"You were young, and you assumed your mother was

telling you the whole truth. You had no reason to doubt her."

"I still regret it, though. And I don't ever want things to be like that between us again."

We hugged, and while things weren't quite back to the way they had been before he'd seen me with Leo, they were headed that way.

"Are you and Leo going to talk more?"

He frowned. "Not today. I need some time first."

"I just want you to know that I'm the one who instigated everything. I pushed him when he said no to being my Dom."

My dad grimaced. "I'm not sure that makes it better, but thank you for telling me."

"I can live with it taking you a while to process things and work out how to be friends with Leo now that we're together. But don't hurt him again like you did yesterday, or me either, or Avery."

"I won't, but I need you to promise not to hide things from me."

"Would you have reacted differently if we'd let you know earlier? We were planning to talk to you today."

"Leo told me that, and I'd like to think I would've taken it better if you had, but I don't know. All I can say for sure is that I'm sorry for not listening to you last night."

We hugged again. "Are you still going to the demo at Succumb today?"

He shook his head. "No, Sean and Blake will be there, but Avery and I are going to go home. There's no way I could go and see Leo and… I just can't."

"I understand, but I hope that you'll forgive Leo completely so things can be like they used to be."

"Minus him telling me all about his latest sub."

"Yeah, I think it's best if you leave his sex life out of your conversations."

He rolled his eyes, and I bumped his shoulder.

"I love you, Dad."

"I love you too, and I'm proud of the man you've become. I'm going to go pick up Avery now. Do you need a ride anywhere?"

I shook my head. "I'm going to hang out here for a little bit longer."

"All right, I'll call you soon."

"Do that." I watched as he walked away, enjoying the sound of the leaves and the cool October breeze.

23

WREN

The next few weeks went by quickly. I had a ton of schoolwork to get through, and I spent all the spare time I had with Leo. Some nights he worked me over in delicious ways, but other nights we just cuddled and rubbed off on each other before falling asleep. I still hadn't gotten brave enough to tell him I loved him, and he apparently wasn't ready to say it out loud either, but he showed me how he felt in the way he cared for me, and the way he listened so intently to everything I said.

He and my dad hadn't talked again, which made me sad. Leo kept reminding me that it really hadn't been that long and that Graham needed time. He said he was okay with that, but I was worried. My dad and I texted periodically, and on my birthday, I went out to dinner with him, Avery, Mandy, Carter, and Felicity. I wanted to bring Leo. If I was dating anyone else, my dad would've included him or her. I told Leo I'd spend the day with him if that was what he wanted, but he told me I was being ridiculous and made me go.

Dinner went fairly smoothly. There were a few

awkward moments when I would've talked about Leo or when my dad would have, and there was still some distance between me and my dad that hadn't been there a few months before. But at least everything felt normal with Avery and my siblings.

Since I was staying overnight, Sean insisted on taking me out. He said he hadn't been out drinking in way too long because Avery was basically an old married man now, so he needed someone to go with who still knew how to have fun. Blake was a saint, driving us from place to place and taking care of us when we were barely capable of staying on our feet. I still wasn't sure how he got us both back to their condo.

I couldn't remember everything that happened that night, but I was absolutely certain Sean and I had a lot of TMI conversations. I might have told him about needle play, and he definitely mentioned something about a tail plug and creative uses for the mirror in their bedroom.

Blake had to put me to bed in their guest room, and he brought me back to life the next day by feeding me bacon, eggs, and toast. As soon as I was clearheaded enough to drive, I hurried home, because I had to get ready for the very best part of my birthday celebration, a scene with Leo where he would pierce my nipples.

Leo and I had talked extensively about piercing and what it would mean—no nipple play for a few months, and a stringent cleaning routine. He'd shown me some options for jewelry, and I'd selected a set of small silver rings. Just thinking about Leo putting them in place had my nipples tingling. It was hard to focus on the road with so much anticipation buzzing through me. This was going to be a great day.

LEO

I PACED MY LIVING ROOM, glancing out the window every time I heard a sound, even though I knew Wren couldn't be here yet. It wasn't like me to be so nervous, and I needed my hands steady and my mind focused for this scene.

I'd worked briefly as a piercer, and I'd done piercing for many other Doms who weren't trained. But I'd never pierced my own sub before, and I hadn't realized how significant it would feel. I wanted everything about this day to be perfect for Wren. Logically, I knew he could always take the rings out if he didn't like them, but no matter how many times I told myself that, it didn't help my nerves.

I checked and rechecked that I had all the supplies I needed for piercing and for the rest of the scene I had planned. Wren was probably expecting us to start with some less intense needle play, but I wanted to do something else. I was guessing he was nervous too, so he needed to focus on something other than needles. I was going to spank him and then give him his first taste of a cane. If he took to it as well as I thought he would, his ass would be stinging as he lay on his back waiting to be pierced, giving him a counterpoint to the pain from the needles.

I forced myself to sit down at my desk and take care of some paperwork for Succumb. Eventually, the frustration of dealing with numerous spreadsheets overrode my nervousness enough that the sound of someone knocking on the door startled me.

"Come in," I called as I pushed back my chair.

Wren opened the door as I entered the living room and he rushed forward, pulling me into a fierce kiss.

"Happy birthday!" I said when we finally came up for air.

"Thank you." Wren smiled, already looking a bit lust drunk.

"Did everything go okay?" I asked.

"Yes, it was all fine until Sean decided tequila shots were a necessary part of any birthday."

"Late night?"

Wren grimaced. "I don't want to talk about it."

"Blake is a saint to put up with that boy."

"He drove us around and took care of us. I owe him."

"Sounds like I do too." I needed to remember to thank him for keeping Wren safe. "How were things with your family?"

"Okay. There were awkward moments, and I really wanted you there, but mostly it felt like it would have a year ago, except there's a whole important part of my life I couldn't talk about."

I nodded. I didn't want to dwell on my issues with Graham, not when Wren and I had been anticipating this scene for what felt like ages, but I also didn't want Wren to think I didn't care. "Do you want to talk more about it?"

"Maybe later or tomorrow, but not right now. I've been thinking about what we're about to do ever since I woke up."

"Have you now?" I said with an evil Dom smile.

He nodded as I gave him a slow once-over. "Strip and position yourself on the spanking bench. I've set it up in the bedroom."

Wren frowned. "Wait, what?"

"You heard me, boy."

"But I thought we were…"

"I am absolutely going to put rings through your very sensitive nipples, but I never said that was all we'd do. You need a warm-up first."

Wren looked like he might protest again, but I

pointed to the bedroom, and he went. I gave him a few minutes so he had time to get naked. When I walked in, my breath caught at the sight of him laid out for me—his dark curls, the gorgeous lines of his back, his pert ass sticking up. "That's perfect, boy. You're just what I need."

"Thank you, Sir."

I smiled, loving how he'd sunk into a more submissive tone, one he only used when he was really into a scene. I felt honored to be gifted with that response. "I thought about just using my hand or a soft flogger on you, something to ease you into our scene, but that's not what I want, and I don't think it would truly please you."

Wren turned to look at me, eyes wide. "What do you want to use?"

I picked up the rattan cane I'd ordered for him, flexed it between my fingers, then swished it through the air. The whistling sound made Wren jump. "I want to cane you, just a few strokes, though. It's very intense for most subs, but I think you need something you really can feel, something to put you in the right headspace to find piercing arousing."

Wren nodded. "Yeah, I… I think I want that."

I swished the cane through the air again, then tapped it against my hand. "You think you can take this for me?"

He licked his lips. "Yes, Sir. I want to."

"And what do you do if you need to stop?"

"I use my safeword."

"Good." I tapped his ass very lightly with the cane. "You can protest all you want: whine, beg, scream. I'll still spank you or cane you however I want unless you say 'red.'"

He shuddered, which was the response I was hoping for, but then he said, "You're so good to me."

My chest tightened. If I'd had any doubt that I loved him, I didn't now. He was everything I wanted and more.

I gave him a soft smile. "Pleasing you is the most important thing to me."

"Thank you," he whispered.

I loved when he let me see how vulnerable he was. I knelt beside him and ran a hand along his back and over his ass. Then I kissed along the path my hand had followed. I knew this experience was going to be even more special than anything that had come before it. I'd feared that what was between me and Wren would fade, that it was all about newness and finding a sub who was well matched with my desire, but my love for him was only growing stronger.

"Wren?"

"Yes?"

"I think I'm in love with you." His eyes widened, and I cleared my throat. "No, that's not right. I don't think it; I know it. I hadn't planned to tell you today. I thought I might risk ruining our scene, but I just realized I needed you to know before you offer me the gift of being the one to pierce you."

Wren sat up, pushing off the bench, and I sank back onto my heels. I was afraid to look at him. What if he was angry or upset, or—

"I love you too. I almost told you the first day we did needle play, but I was scared you'd think it was ridiculous for me to feel so much so fast."

"It is fast, but... your dad taught me that fast doesn't mean it's not real."

Wren smiled. "Yeah, I didn't believe in love at first sight until I got to know Avery and saw him with my dad."

"So... um... did I ruin the moment or..." *Please let him say he still wants this—the cane, the piercing, me.*

He shook his head, and I held my breath. "No, you made it better."

He stood and repositioned himself over the spanking bench. "Knowing that you're doing this to me because you love me and you know it's what I crave makes it even hotter."

His words filled me with hope that we really did have a future. "I love how well you understand this dynamic between us, because this really is all about pleasing you. I love being a Dom. I love spanking subs, flogging them, sticking needles in their skin, but more than anything else I love being able to make someone feel exquisite, and with you, the man I love, it all feels like so much more than it's ever been with anyone else."

Wren relaxed against the bench and wriggled his ass. "So please me already."

"Brat." I secured his wrists and ankles. Then I began with a light spanking, slowly putting more force behind the blows until Wren was starting to shift away from them, and each blow forced a small whimper from him.

I changed things up then, sometimes giving a barely there tap and other times a hard slap that echoed in the room. Soon Wren was bucking his hips, trying to get some friction on his cock. His breath came in pants as I smacked his now nicely red ass.

I paused and ran my hands over the heated flesh. "How do you feel?"

He groaned. "Good. Sore. Needy."

"I like all of that. Are you ready to try the cane?"

He took a deep breath, and I watched as his sides expanded. He let the air out with a whoosh as I swished the cane through the air, making a vicious noise.

"Bastard," Wren said, shivering.

I chuckled. "Just you wait."

I tapped his ass lightly with the cane, then a little harder. He gave a very satisfying shout when I laid the first real blow across his ass cheeks. I followed it immediately with another, pulling away quickly to really make it sting.

"Fuck! Too much. It's too much." Wren squirmed against the bench, pulling on the restraints.

"I know it's hard, baby, but I want to give you five more. Can you take that?"

He drew in a shaky breath as I rubbed my hand up and down his back, trying to soothe him.

"Yes, Sir. I can."

"Good boy." I patted his ass, then caned him twice in quick succession. He cried out, twisting away from the cane. I rubbed his back again, and then slid my fingers into his hair, massaging his scalp. He looked up at me, his dark eyes filled with pain, but also with something more, something I thought was love.

I pulled away and hit him again, not quite as hard this time. He breathed through it.

"Good boy. You're doing so good. Just two more." I reached underneath him and worked his cock. It was rock hard and leaking precum, which made me smile.

I let go of him and brought the cane down on the back of his thighs.

He cried out. "Fuck. God. Fuck. That stings."

"Remember how it feels when I send the needle through your nipples. You can compare the pain."

"Fuck you."

I whipped the cane down on his ass one last time, making him sob. "Too much, Leo. Please."

I sat the cane aside and knelt, releasing his restraints. "It's okay, baby. This part is all over. And your ass looks so beautiful all striped and red."

"Th-thank you." Wren's voice cracked as tears ran down his face.

I helped him off the bench and pulled him onto my lap. "Talk to me. Are you okay?"

"Yes," he sniffled. "I mean it hurts, but it's good. Thank you."

"You're welcome, baby." I held him as he cried softly against my shoulder.

When his tears had stopped, I kissed the side of his head. "You needed this release, didn't you?"

He nodded. "Yes. I didn't know how much."

"Come on, let's get you on the bed." I kept my arm around him, knowing he would be shaky as I led him to the bed and helped him lie down on his back.

"My ass hurts." His pouty look was fucking adorable.

"That is kind of the point."

"Bastard."

"Yes, I am."

He closed his eyes and sighed as he deliberately rubbed his sore ass on the sheets.

"Are you ready for more?"

He looked down at his nipples and nodded. "Yes, Sir."

"Stretch your arms over your head. I've got everything ready."

I was so glad I'd talked to him about aftercare for the piercing already. We'd negotiated everything for this scene before he left for Asheville, so he already knew exactly what would happen. Now all he had to do was relax and feel.

24

WREN

I watched Leo readying his supplies. My ass ached, but the pain felt distant. The cane had hurt worse than anything we'd done before. And I'd loved it. I might have come if Leo had pushed me any further. I resisted the urge to rub my ass against the bed again. I knew I was full of endorphins, and I'd probably regret aggravating the welts when I came back down.

I exhaled, sinking into the mattress. Every part of me felt relaxed except for my cock, which desperately wanted some attention. I knew it wasn't going to get any until after Leo put the rings in, though.

I wanted to ask a question, but it took me a few tries before I could make words come out. "Can I see the needles?" I knew they were larger, but I wanted to see if I could tell the difference. He held up a packaged one for me to see.

"Holy shit! Those are *a lot* thicker."

"They are, but you can handle it."

They were really going to hurt, but people who didn't even like pain did this every day, so I knew Leo was right. I could take it, but I was hoping to actually like it, and I wasn't sure that would happen.

Leo snapped the cuffs into place, restraining my wrists and ankles. Then he ran a soothing hand over my leg. "Just because we're doing this as a scene doesn't mean you have to like it. You may not find any pleasure in this, and that is okay."

I nodded. "I know. Even if I don't, doing it like this, with me restrained and you being the one to put the rings in, it's so… intimate."

He smiled. "It is."

"Are you going to let me come when it's over?"

"Maybe."

"Leooooo."

He grinned. "Let's see how you feel then, okay?"

I glanced down at my dick. "I don't think I'm going to feel any less horny."

He gripped me, working my cock with his fist. I arched up, and the ache in my ass made me gasp.

"No," Leo said. "I don't really think you are, either, no matter how badly this hurts."

"I want you to come afterwards too."

He gave one last tug on my cock. "Yes, that will definitely be happening."

I watched as he pulled on gloves and then opened an alcohol swab. He cleaned my right nipple, and I managed not to yelp at the cold. He kissed me gently before opening a needle and readying it. My heart rate sped up, and I wasn't sure I knew how to breathe anymore.

"I… I think I have to close my eyes."

"That's fine, baby. Do you want me to keep going?"

"Yes. Please."

"Okay, you do whatever you need to. You don't have to watch."

I nodded, eyes now firmly closed.

He pinched my nipple, and I tensed as he toyed with it, rolling it, stretching it. "One. Two." He drove the needle in without ever saying three.

I screamed. "Shit. Fuck. Shit. That hurts."

"I know, baby. I'm attaching the ring to the needle now, and I'm going to pull it back through."

"Oh, fuck." I braced myself, but I still hissed and whined as he pulled the ring through.

"You did so good, and it looks great on you, even better than I expected."

I shuddered, trying to get away from the pain. But that only made my ass sting. He'd known that was how it would work; trying to escape one pain just caused another. "You're evil."

He chuckled as he cleaned me up. I hoped there wasn't much blood. He hadn't expected there to be. I opened my eyes, needing to see him. "Look at your ring, boy."

I did, and fuck me, there really was a silver ring running through my nipple. This was real. And now Leo was going to do the other one.

I sucked in my breath when he pinched my other nipple. "Close your eyes and take a deep breath."

"There's no point in counting, since I can't trust you with it." I sounded like a total brat, but I didn't care.

"I won't bother then." He tortured my nipple while I tried to slow my breathing. Then, just as I exhaled a huge breath, he pierced it.

I cried out, bucking up. If I hadn't been restrained, I might've shoved him away. He quickly pulled the ring through, and it was all over.

"You did so good, boy," he assured me as he cleaned me up. "You can look now."

First I looked at Leo like I had before. He was smiling

as he surveyed at his work. "They're perfect. I can't wait until we can play with them."

I looked at them then, and I knew once they healed I would love having him use them to torture me. And no matter how much they hurt or how scared I'd been, my dick had never gone soft. I was restrained in Leo's bed, with endorphins coursing through me, and suddenly all I could think of was sex. I wanted to thank Leo in the best way I could imagine.

"Leo?"

"Yes, baby?"

"I want to suck you."

He frowned. "I'm not sure that's—"

"I want you to straddle my face, hold onto the headboard, and feed me your cock, so I can thank you."

His eyes widened, and he nodded. "Okay. Just hang on." He quickly finished cleaning up, and then, clearly being very careful not to touch my nipples, he did exactly what I'd asked.

I opened my mouth as he undid his pants, and once his cock was free, he drove into my mouth, not giving me any mercy. I gagged and sputtered around him. He pulled back long enough to let me take in some air, and then pushed in again, fucking my mouth like he owned me.

My nipples burned, my ass ached, my throat was full of his cock, and I was so fucking happy. Giving him that much control over my body had me so hot that when he gave a shout and started coming down my throat, I came too.

Leo carefully maneuvered off me and licked at the cum that had run from my mouth.

"So fucking gorgeous," he muttered, and even if I hadn't been able to see him, I would've known he was smiling.

He freed me from the restraints, climbed into bed, and leaned back against the headboard, so I could fit myself between his legs.

I took one of his hands and laced our fingers together. "I love you. Thank you for doing this for me."

"I love you too, and doing this was an honor. I'll think about how much I love you every time I see these rings."

"This is the best birthday present ever."

Leo kissed the top of my head. "I'm so glad I got to share this with you and that you pushed me to acknowledge how much I want you."

I hoped he wasn't too disappointed that he didn't get to share in all of my birthday celebration.

As if he knew what I was thinking, he gripped my chin, turning me to look at him. "Everything will work out for us, okay?"

"You seem so sure of yourself."

"It's hard not to be after what we just did."

We both laughed, and I relaxed into him, enjoying the feel of him petting my hair and thankful I didn't have to do anything but lie there with him for the rest of the day.

25

LEO

The Friday before Thanksgiving, I was working on some paperwork in my office at Succumb. I was rechecking some figures that didn't look right to me when my phone rang. I almost ignored it, but thinking it might be Wren needing to change our plans for the evening, I glanced at the screen. It was Graham.

"Hello?"

"Hi, Leo. I… um… shit. I've almost called you so many times, but I've been too much of a fucking coward to follow through, and now there's something I really need to talk through with a friend. You're the one I've always talked to. I want your advice, but…"

"When I was trying to decide whether it was wrong for me to go out with Wren, one of the hardest things was not being able to talk to you. I always ask you about any tough decisions I have to make, and I share the good and bad things in my life, and not being able to… well, it sucks."

"Yeah, it does."

I closed my laptop and stood up from my desk, so I could stretch. "I'm here to listen."

"Really, even after I was such a hypocrite?"

"I meant what I said. I don't want to lose our friendship."

"I'm actually in Charlotte. If you wanted to get together for coffee or something stronger…"

"I would like that a lot. Meet at Jim's in an hour? I've been craving their cheese fries all week."

Graham responded with a smile in his voice. "That sounds perfect."

I quickly texted Wren to explain what was up and that we'd have to meet a little later than planned. He was too happy about his dad calling me to care.

"So what's up?" I asked Graham as I slid into a booth across from him. We'd both gotten drinks at the bar and then found an out-of-the-way spot where we could talk.

"First, I want to say that there's no rational reason for me to object to your relationship with Wren, and I'd like you to join us for Thanksgiving."

I'd been putting off solidifying my Thanksgiving plans, because I didn't want Wren to miss spending the day with his family, but he'd been insisting he wanted to be with me instead. I hadn't expected Graham to be ready to have me at a family gathering. "You really want me there? With your whole family?"

"You're part of my family, Leo, and the rest of them have all been encouraging me to ask you. I've just been too stubborn."

"Can you actually believe I feel the same way about Wren that you feel about Avery?" It was important to me that he truly accepted our relationship for what it was, that he knew it wasn't something temporary.

Graham nodded. "I do. I think this would be a lot harder for me if I didn't."

"Then I'll be there for Thanksgiving." My voice was so choked with emotion, I barely got the words out.

Graham took a shaky breath. "You've done so much for me over the last eight years. I know it sounds melodramatic, but you truly did save me. I was a fucking mess when I left Louise."

"True, but you were an interesting fucking mess. I'm really glad I was able to help you."

"You were the only family I had for years. You know that, right?"

I nodded, unable to speak, because I was about to cry right there in public.

We both sipped our beers and took a few moments to compose ourselves. When I could trust my voice again, I said, "We're a pretty fucked-up family, with you dating your daughter-in-law's best friend and me dating your son."

Graham huffed. "And Sean and Blake are coming to Thanksgiving too. Sean can always be counted on for added insanity."

I grinned. "It will be a very interesting day."

"Yes it will." He paused for a moment. Then, looking more serious, he said, "Thank you for forgiving me."

"Thank you for accepting that I love your son. Now, what did you need to talk to me about?"

"I want to propose to Avery."

I set my beer down, glad I hadn't actually taken a sip.

"You do?" I shouldn't have been surprised, but I'd expected him to wait until Christmas or maybe Valentine's.

"I was thinking I'd do it at Thanksgiving dinner with everyone there, but I want to be sure I'm not crazy. I don't want him to be angry that we aren't alone, or feel so much pressure that he... I don't know. I just thought—"

"Graham, I think that's a beautiful idea, and I don't think there's any chance he won't say yes."

"Really?"

Was he serious? "Yes, really."

"Can we talk through my plan?"

"Of course."

We did, and the longer we sat there, the more our friendship felt exactly like it had for the last eight years... comfortable, like we'd known each other always, like the best kind of family.

My HEART POUNDED as Wren and I walked up Graham and Avery's porch steps. Even though things were better between me and Graham, I was still worried about awkward moments, about everyone else's reactions, and about Graham's plans. I really hoped I hadn't steered Graham wrong.

Wren knocked on the door, and Graham opened it almost immediately and hugged each of us in turn. I hadn't told Wren about the proposal plans, because Graham wanted to be the one to do that.

I said, "Since you two haven't seen each other in a while, why don't I step on in and give you a few moments together." Wren looked at me suspiciously, but I gave him a reassuring smile.

When I stepped inside, I noticed that Felicity and her mother had taken over the kitchen. Wren's sister, Mandy, was talking to Blake, and Sean and Avery were standing close together whispering. Blake kept glancing at them as if trying to decide if he needed to head off any trouble.

Wren's brother, Carter, was watching everyone with a smile on his face. I realized I was too. This was exactly the kind of family Thanksgiving I'd longed for growing up.

A few moments later, Graham and Wren came inside, and the smile on Wren's face told me their conversation had gone well. Wren walked over and took my hand. "Did everyone interrogate you while I was out there?"

I shook my head. "No, they all seem to just accept me being here."

"They should. You've been like family to my dad for a long time."

I supposed I had, and I was glad things felt like that again. I gestured to all the food that was laid out on the kitchen island. "This is quite a spread."

Wren frowned. "Hey, Dad, if Leo and I brought the wine and beer, what did these two do?" He inclined his head toward Avery and Sean. "Avery said they can't cook any better than I can."

Graham winced. "No. I wouldn't even trust them to open canned cranberry sauce."

Sean grinned. "Actually, I have a really funny story about Avery and a can opener."

Avery punched his arm. "Don't you dare."

Graham rolled his eyes at their antics. "Avery cleaned the house."

"Sean entertained me while I did the cooking," Blake added. "That was the best contribution I could think of for him."

"That does sound about right," Avery said, and I could imagine the kind of entertainment he'd provided. If I knew Blake, he'd probably had the boy restrained and kneeling on the kitchen floor.

"Don't worry," Graham said. "Only competent people were allowed to do the actual cooking. Blake made mashed potatoes and bacon-wrapped asparagus. Felicity and Carter made a fruit salad and macaroni and cheese. Felicity's mom is providing dessert. And I made the rest."

A timer rang, and Graham rushed into the kitchen to pull a pan of rolls from the oven.

"Wow, are those homemade?" Mandy asked.

Graham nodded. "They are."

She huffed. "You never made homemade bread when we were kids."

"I didn't know how then. I only started baking recently."

Mandy narrowed her eyes. "Then I expect to see some more of it. No more holding out on us."

"You think you should be getting deliveries of fresh bread each week or something?"

She seemed to consider that. "I'd be willing to come pick it up."

Everyone laughed at that. Then Felicity grabbed a fork and tapped it against a wine glass. Once she had everyone's attention, she told us to grab our plates, fill them, and head to the table.

"Do we have assigned seats?" Sean asked.

"No, but if we did you would've been put at the kids' table," she said.

He flipped her off. "You know I'd sit wherever I wanted anyway."

Blake smacked Sean's ass. "Behave, boy."

His action earned him a "wooooo" from Avery, and Felicity clanged her fork on the glass again. "I could just pack up all this food and take it home."

"All right, everybody. That's enough," Carter said. "Do what she says. I really want to eat."

Finally, we started moving in the right direction. Plates

got overfilled, drinks were poured, and we all managed to find a place to sit.

They'd added leaves to the table and pushed a smaller table up to one end. Some people were basically in the living room, which was separated from the dining room by an open, arched doorway. But we were all there, one crazy, fucked-up family that I was honored to be part of.

When Graham stood and asked for silence, my heart rate accelerated. I knew what was coming next, and it was no ordinary toast. "Today I'm thankful for family and for friends who've become family." He glanced at me. Wren squeezed my thigh, and warmth spread through my chest. I couldn't remember ever having a better holiday than this one.

Graham continued. "A year ago, I never imagined being where I am right now, so happy and filled with love. Each of you have contributed to that, but Avery especially has taught me what true love really is."

I glanced at Avery and saw tears shining in his eyes. Graham turned to face him then. "Avery, I love you deeply." He walked around the table and knelt by Avery's chair.

"What? What are you doing?" Avery asked.

"I'm hoping you'll agree to be my husband, so I can spend the rest of our lives showing you how much you mean to me." He pulled out a ring box and opened it. Inside was a silver band with a crushed amethyst inlay. It was perfect for Avery.

Tears ran down Avery's cheeks as he stared at Graham, wide-eyed.

Sean thumped Avery on the shoulder. "You're supposed to answer him."

"Oh... I... Yes!"

Graham pulled Avery into his arms as we all clapped, many of us needing to wipe away tears of our own.

After Graham slipped the ring onto Avery's finger, I stood and held up my glass. "To Graham and Avery! Happy Thanksgiving!"

Everyone began clinking glasses and wishing Graham and Avery a happy future together. Eventually we set our drinks down and began to eat. There was laughter, there was love, and Wren was right beside me. Most people were moving on to dessert before I'd even eaten half my food, because I spent so much time just watching the man who'd captured my heart.

After partaking of the amazing desserts Felicity's mom had made, everyone helped clear the table. Sean and Blake insisted on loading the dishwasher. A few of the others headed out on a walk, and I took Wren's hand and led him onto the porch. We sat down on the bench swing and spent a few moments enjoying the quiet.

"Avery told me the porch and especially this swing was what made him fall in love with the house," I said.

"I can see why. This probably sounds ridiculous, but this house has a good vibe to it. I want to design houses that make people feel like this one does."

I put my arm around him and pulled him against me. "I know you will."

Another few moments passed in silence, then Wren said, "I can't believe my dad and Avery are really engaged."

"I'm happy for them."

"Me too—and everything's really okay between you and my dad?"

I nodded. "Yes. I think we'll need to work on establishing some boundaries, but I'm confident now that I can have Graham as a friend, and you as…" What was the right label for us? "A boyfriend? A partner?"

"So this is an exclusive thing?"

I bit back a growl. "Damn right it is. I don't want anyone but you, Wren. I've never said 'I love you' to another man before, and"—I knew this was probably too much too soon, but I said it anyway—"I can't imagine ever saying it to anyone else. You're it for me."

He smiled. "I feel the same way. You're my everything."

I gave him a quick kiss, conscious that Graham could return from his walk any minute. "You're the thing I'm most thankful for today."

He grinned at me. "Remember when I told you I didn't want any Dom but you, and you tried to tell me how wrong I was?"

"I thought you were just being stubborn."

"That was me telling you that, despite how ridiculous it might seem, despite how little experience I'd had, I knew you were the one for me."

I kissed him again, forcing myself to pull back well before I wanted to. His eyes were bright, and he looked so damn happy. "I have plans for you."

"Oh really? What do those plans entail?"

I looked him up and down. "Sadly, your nipples aren't ready to be played with, but we still haven't tried out that inflatable butt plug I ordered."

Wren licked his lips. "The one that's already huge before it even inflates?"

"That's the one."

"Maybe we should go ahead and say our goodbyes?"

I smiled at him. "Soon, baby. Very soon."

Dear Reader,

Thank you for downloading *Painfully Attractive*. I hope you enjoyed it. If you haven't read the rest of the Love and Care series, it starts with *Father of the Groom* and continues with *After the Weekend* and *Demanding Discipline*. If you like May/December romance you may also enjoy the *Thorne and Dash* series which starts with *Professional Distance.* I offer a free book to anyone who joins my mailing list. To learn more, go to silviaviolet.com/newsletter.

Please consider leaving a review where you purchased this ebook or on Goodreads. Reviews and word-of-mouth recommendations are vital to independent authors.

I love hearing from readers. You can chat with me on Facebook in Silvia's Salon, and you can email me at silviaviolet@gmail.com. To read excerpts from all of my titles, visit my website: silviaviolet.com/books.

Silvia Violet

ABOUT THE AUTHOR

Silvia Violet writes fun, sexy stories that will leave you smiling and satisfied. She has a thing for characters who are in need of comfort and enjoys helping them surrender to love even when they doubt it exists. Silvia's stories include sizzling contemporaries, paranormals, and historicals. When she needs a break from listening to the voices in her head, she spends time baking, taking long walks, curling up with her favorite books, and hanging out with her family.

- Website: silviaviolet.com
- Facebook Group: Silvia's Salon
- Facebook: facebook.com/silvia.violet
- Bookbub: bookbub.com/profile/silvia-violet
- Instagram: @silvia.violet
- Twitter: @Silvia_Violet
- Pinterest: silviaviolet

ALSO BY SILVIA VIOLET

Three Under the Christmas Tree

Needing A Little Christmas

Lace-Covered Compromise

A Chance at Love

Coming Clean

If Wishes Were Horses

Revolutionary Temptation

Of Hope and Anguish

Love and Care

Father of the Groom

After the Weekend

Demanding Discipline

Fitting In

Fitting In

Sorting Out

Burning Up

Going Deep

Getting Hitched

Thorne and Dash

Professional Distance

Personal Entanglement

36241829R00115

Printed in Poland
by Amazon Fulfillment
Poland Sp. z o.o., Wrocław